Chanekka Pullens Publishing Presents

Misuse

Book Of Stories

By Rosa James

Parental Advisory Advised

Contact Information:

Email: misuselsnake@gmail.com

Misuse: Book Of Stories

Books may be purchased in quantity by contacting the author by email at: misuselsnakes@gmail.com with 'Book Purchase' in the subject line.

ISBN: 978-0-578-34439-3

1. Erotic Fiction

Printed in the USA

STORY ONE

MY BROTHERS KEEPER

TABLE OF CONTENTS

FRESH OUT: DECECMBER 2017

Alex walked out the gates of the Federal Correctional Institution in Texarkana, Texas and took in the fresh air. After sharing close quarters with other men for the past twelve years and six months, the little things mattered like the cool crisp December air against his face. He kneeled and literally kissed the ground before standing back up.

"Thank you, God! I made it out!" he yelled, looking up to the partly cloudy sky.

"See you when you get back," said the officer, securing the prison gate.

Alex didn't pay the officer any mind as he headed to the black Lincoln Navigator that waited for him by the curb. When he opened the door and hopped inside the passenger seat, his younger brother, Wyatt, greeted him while handing over a cigar stuffed with weed.

"Brother, let's get the fuck out of here. I never want to plant a foot on this property again. On the real, I was going to make you walk to the end of the block. But then, I was like nah that nigga did over a decade so just pull up to the door. Anyway, welcome home, big bro! Now, let's go get that prison smell off you," joked Wyatt, pressing the gas and speeding out the parking lot of the prison.

Wyatt drove two blocks before looking over at Alex who was inhaling and exhaling the weed.

"Man, this that good shit. I was so tired of that trash the prison officers were sneaking inside," said Alex.

Wyatt laughed. "Brother, you are seriously off your game." He sped up, noticing a chicken spot halfway up the road.

"What are you talking about, bro?" he questioned, looking over at him.

He gave his brother a sarcastic look before looking at the rearview mirror. When Alex turned and looked, there sat a young woman wearing nothing. He smiled as he admired the woman's long jet-black weave, dark chocolate silky skin, and full lips. Her makeup was flawless, and her c-cup breast sat up perfect with no support.

"Brother, you know just the way I love them," he said before handing Wyatt the cigar and diving into the backseat to join the woman.

Without hesitating, the woman reached into his prison sweats, releasing his manhood and wrapped her warm mouth around it.

Wyatt pulled into the parking lot of the chicken spot and parked. He looked back. "Hey, I know food might be the last thing on your mind, but do you two want anything? I heard about this spot from a friend."

"No, brother, we will … we will … get something later!" answered Alex, trying not to moan like a bitch.

He chuckled and got out the SUV. He entered the restaurant, ordered his food, sat, and ate. When he returned a half hour later, Alex was hitting the girl doggie style. Unnoticed, Wyatt started the SUV, turned the radio up loud, and headed to the motel.

Ten minutes later, they arrived at the motel and Wyatt parked the SUV. He opened the glove compartment and grabbed two keys before turning around.

"Hey, brother, here is the key to your room. It's next door to mines. Our flight leaves tomorrow afternoon, so go inside, tighten up, and let me know if you want to get out later tonight to hit up some places."

He tossed the room key along with a band of money in the backseat. He exited the car with plans to call his woman, Denise, and get some rest.

Once Alex busted his nut, he and the woman dressed and exited the SUV. When they made it to the motel room, he went for round two and three before taking a rest and ordering some food. He sent the woman across the way to grab some Hennessey while waiting for the food to be delivered.

Once the food arrived, they shared a meal, had drinks, and watched the movie *Paid in Full* before continuing their sex escapade for the remainder of the night.

The next afternoon, Wyatt and Alex had brunch before saying goodbye to the woman and heading to the Texarkana Regional Airport. They were to fly back home to their hometown of Baton City, Missouri.

Hours later, Alex exited the plane and took in the cold Baton City air before yelling, "Killer City, I am back to claim my throne now!"

Everyone looked at him, but he did not care as he continued to follow Wyatt to claim his bag.

"Hey, brother, you better chill before these TSA motherfuckers think you on some terrorist shit," joked Wyatt as they exited the airport.

Their brother Duncan was waiting by the curb, arguing with the security guard. "See, there are my brothers, so can you get off my back now!" Duncan yelled, walking away from the security guard, clapping his hands.

"This nigga been out here tripping with me for the past five minutes and I was not moving until you two came out," Duncan spoke while hugging Alex. He broke his embrace and took a step back to give his big brother a once over. "Okay, I see you all swollen and shit! Those photos didn't do any justice, they made you look chubby. But in person, your ass is ripped! I guess there was one benefit of prison." He joked as they headed to the car.

"So, I see my younger twin brothers have hell of jokes," said Alex.

Wyatt tossed his bag in the trunk, the three got inside the car, then they drove away.

A half hour later, Duncan parked in front of Wyatt's downtown loft so that Alex could shower and put on the new clothing that Wyatt picked out for him a week ago.

"Man, thanks, brother. You had my clothes laid out on the bed in the guest room like it was the first day of school and shit. I owe you when I get back on my feet. You have been outstanding holding it down while I did my time," said Alex, admiring himself in the mirror.

"Come on now, remember, I am my brother's keeper," responded Wyatt, having a drink at the bar.

"Okay, man, you look great. But we need to head out. The family is waiting for you, and I want to get some of momma's oxtails before my greedy sons eat them up," Duncan said, heading to the front door.

Wyatt laughed. "Man, Alex, wait until you see your nephews Banks and Adams. They are damn near big as you. Your nephew Evan is doing his thang as well. He is taking some classes at Baton Community College until he figures out what he wants to do."

After finishing his drink, Wyatt and Alex exited the building. Duncan was parked out front waiting with the car running. When they got inside, Duncan was on the phone checking to made sure there were still some oxtails.

"Banks, just put me a plate up. We on our way now!" Duncan hung up the phone, put the car in drive, and drove away.

"Man, you still don't play about your food," joked Alex as he sat comfortably in the heated seats of the BMW.

The brothers shared a laugh. For the remainder of the ride, they caught Alex up on the latest in the city.

"Man, that nigga Kay'Ron came up. But he lost his bitch Roxanne. Do you remember her?" questioned Duncan, never taking his eyes off the road.

"Yeah, I remember Roxanne, she was a down ass little girl, real solid," responded Alex, looking out of the passenger side window.

"Man, that shit was sad. She was pregnant and everything and someone killed her. Put her in the trunk of her own car. If you ask me, I think it was his hating ass uncle, Marvin," spoke Wyatt, checking his text messages.

"Yeah, that nigga Marvin was always a bitch. Remember he used to get his ass kicked in the projects. But his pops, David, and sister, Natty, were beasts out here," said Alex.

"We are here, and I am ready to eat," said Duncan, parking the car in the driveway.

Alex hurried out the car and entered his mother's house.

"Surprise!" everyone yelled as Rose hurried over to her son.

She began hugging him before pulling his face down to hers and planting kisses on his cheek. "Come on over to this table and get you some real food. I cooked everything you like!" said Rose, guiding her son to the dining room table.

Alex sat at the head of the table while Rose piled different food on his plate. Everyone ate, had drinks, and enjoyed each other's company for the next few hours. When most of the family and friends were gone, Alex joined his brothers and nephews in the den.

When he entered and looked around the room, he smiled observing his family happy and enjoying each other's company. His nephews Adams, Banks, and Evans played the video game while Duncan and Wyatt were debating about celebrities and fake asses. All the brothers were in attendance except for the oldest, James.

Suddenly the door opened, and James entered.

"Well, look what the skunk dragged in," kidded Duncan.

James gave him a silly look. "Well, do skunks drag in these!" He held up a sack of Kush in one hand, and a three liters of Remy Martin VSOP in the other.

"Hey, dad!" said Evans before returning to the video game.

"Hey, son, Adams, Banks," responded James as he walked over to Alex. He looked at his little brother for several seconds. "Man, I still can't believe you are standing here in the flesh!" He hugged him before handing him the bottle of liquor.

"Now, let's get this party started. I have all my brothers here, our next generation is here, I am at momma's house, and I already had some pussy. So, I am Gucci at the moment!" yelled Alex before laughing. He opened the bottle, taking a drink.

For the next few hours, the brothers drank and reminisced about the days when they were hustling in the streets. After sharing many memories and joking around, Alex was ready to get back to the beat of things.

"Man, those were the days. So, now that we are all here and then some, when are we getting back to the money?" questioned Alex in a serious voice.

Duncan and James looked at each other and shook their heads while Wyatt gulped down the remaining liquor in his glass.

Evans paused the video game and turned to his uncle. "Uncle Alex, I heard you guys were heavy back in the day. People in my generation still talk about all of you. Uncle Alex, you are a legend out here," he finished, focusing back on the video game.

Evans's comment gave Alex a boost of self-esteem. He knew that if he were still considered a legend, then it would take no time for him to get back to the street money.

"Don't worry, nephew, we about to be back on now that I'm home." He looked around at his brothers who did not seem excited about it.

He could see the doubt in all three of their faces. "So, what's up my brother's keeper? I'm home. Now, we can get back on track like before."

Wyatt spoke, "Brother, I still hustle, and I am down for whatever; but we have to be careful because these new niggas are soft. They will hate on you and snitch all at the same time." He warned.

"Brother, fuck all that! Niggas been snitching since the fifties! We can handle that punk shit. I am aware that shit isn't like it used to be, but that won't stop us from getting back on top. I mean don't get me wrong, you seem like you well off, Wyatt. But we can always do better; shit, we are in our thirties now! Let's show these young ass niggas how it's done."

James stood from his seat and headed to the bar to pour another drink. "For one, nigga, you still saying 'scoop'. How the fuck you going to catch up with the new shit going on out here when your slang is still from the early nineties? But on some real shit, when the bust happened years ago, after paying the lawyer to shave some of the years off your time, and tying up some loose ends, we just divided everything up and walked away from the streets."

"Okay, so where is my cut then?" questioned Alex, his palms now itching.

"It's at the crib in the safe, fam. It's only fifty thousand," responded Wyatt.

"Okay, that's enough to get me on. I have a supplier set up. So, who's in?" Alex inquired.

Everyone looked at each other. Wyatt spoke first, "You know I am always down for the hustle. I just needed a partner." He gave Alex dap followed by a hug.

"I opt out. Plus, I put all my money in my barbershop and a couple investments. I'm keeping my hands clean. I lost my wife to that street shit, and I never want my boys to feel the pain of losing another parent," Duncan said.

"I can respect that, brother," responded Alex, giving Duncan dap.

"The dealership is doing good for me, so I'm cool. Besides, I promised Carmen I was going to keep my hands clean," said James.

Alex observed Evans giving his father a sarcastic look and he made a mental note to check that out later.

"Well, I guess it's just me and you, Wyatt!" stated Alex.

Wyatt shrugged. "Well, that's all we need. So, let's get this money so I can quit half ass working at this damn factory."

Everyone laughed at Wyatt's comment. They spent the rest of the night joking and reminiscing with each other until Rose had enough and made everyone go home.

FATHER'S DAY: JUNE 2018

Alex drove down the street with the roof down in his brand new royal blue 2019 Camaro, sitting on 24-inch rims. The June sun was hot, but he didn't mind because it was his first summer out. He slowed down and parked in front of Duncan's barbershop, hopped out, and headed towards the door. When he entered, Banks was sweeping the hair from the floor while Adams cut his father's hair.

"I see you, nephew. You have skills," said Alex, observing Duncan's fresh cut.

"Thanks, Uncle Alex!" he responded, lining the back of his father's neck.

"When he is done, I got you, brother," Duncan said, sitting still.

"I know you do. I shouldn't have never let you convince me to cut my hair off, man. Now I have to work harder to get in between the ladies' legs," joked Alex, taking a seat.

"Damn, Uncle Alex, that car is not set to release until September! How did you get one?" questioned Banks. Alex tossed the keys over to him before responding, "I have my ways, nephew. Why don't you take the whip for a spin and catch you some little girls." Alex went over to take a seat in Duncan's chair.

Excited, Adams dangled the keys. "Bet, I will be back in an hour! Man, wait until the girls see me in this." He checked himself in the mirror.

Banks came out the back room after putting the cleaning supplies away. "Pops, can Adams drop me off at the drama club? It's open mic night."

Before Duncan could respond, Alex spoke, "You would rather go to the drama club instead of rolling around with your bro catching chicks in a hot car?"

Duncan tried to intervene again, but Alex held his hand up. "Hold on, Duncan, I want to hear his answer."

"Uncle Alex, it's not that. It's just I want a classy girl, so, I go to classy places to find them. The drama club is the perfect place," responded Banks with a devilish smile.

They all three shared a laugh before Banks exited the barbershop. Adams was already waiting with the car running.

"You know Banks is gay right?" said Alex.

Duncan, who was now cleaning the clippers, looked up at him in the mirror. "Now what was gay about his answer?"

"Trust me, brother, after spending twelve years in prison, I know gay when I see it. And what teenage boy with hormones want a classy girl right now? When I was fifteen years old, I was trying to sow all my wild oats and I wanted the nastiest girl. I mean, miss Jackson nasty, you feel me?" he finished, laughing at the memory of himself as a young man.

"Brother, I think you got it wrong. These new generation of kids are different," responded Duncan, no longer wanting to entertain the conversation.

"No, this new generation is gay as fuck," countered Alex.

Trying to avoid the subject, Duncan changed it. "So, it looks like the game has been treating you well, my brother."

"Brother, you are absolutely correct. It's like I never left. That supplier I found in prison been coming through with the best of the best. I'm putting these local bums out," he bragged.

"Yeah, I know you are. Hell, you have become the talk of the barbershop. That's why I added you to my personal appointments on Sundays and Mondays when the barbershop should be closed. You are now a part of my high-risk clientele that need minimum mix and mingle. You watch yourself out here. This new breed of niggas is mad at you and cutthroat, so stay all the way woke," warned Duncan.

"Don't worry, little brother. I'm not worried about these niggas. After spending all those years in prison, death does not even scare me. I will live every moment of my life like it's my last because I lost years of it."

"Brother, I hated that shit went down like that for real," said Duncan, paying extra attention to Alex's line.

"Aye, don't worry about it. That's the past. And I was the only one able to do the time. You and James had kids. And I knew Wyatt was going to look out for me while I was down, so I sacrificed myself."

Duncan nodded in agreement and finished cutting Alex's hair. They sat and talked shit until Adams came back an hour and a half later.

Adams came in the barbershop excited. "Hey, Unc, I caught so many chicks, you have to let me take this out again and get more time! Maybe to Baton Park?" He tossed the keys to Alex and went to the back.

"Don't worry, nephew, I got you. Besides, I plan to change up soon anyway. I've been eyeing something classic to put on these streets!" Alex yelled to Adams. He was now focusing on the picture of Duncan's late wife, Trina, on the mirror and shaking his head.

"Brother, I hate what happened to their mother. She was such a good woman and didn't deserve that. I miss my little sis." He handed Duncan a Benjamin.

Feeling sad, Duncan spoke, "Brother, what happened to her is one of the reasons why I refuse to get back in the game. Man, Trina would have rolled with me until the wheels fell off. These niggas couldn't stand to see a down as woman like that, so they took her from me." He was holding out four twenty-dollar bills to Alex.

"Nah, keep the change, brother. We're good. Hey, remember when Trina went with me to shoot them niggas on the northeast side of town that was talking shit. She was six months pregnant with Banks and Adams!" Alex laughed.

"I know. Her ass was supposed to be on bedrest, talking about she had to go help her big brother and shit!" He looked at the picture of his wife. "They don't make them like Trina anymore. The boys were only seven years old when we lost her, and it's been rough without her." He took a seat in his barber chair.

"I caught up with those niggas that did that shit in prison. We are going to cherish her memory. But with all due respect, Duncan, I need to get you in the Camaro so you can get some pussy. I have been watching and have yet to see a bitch on your hills. Little bro, it won't hurt to get out here and mingle or get some pussy," joked Alex, heading to the door.

Adams came from the back, joining the conversation. "Uncle Alex, I tried to tell him. Please take him somewhere. All he does is work and stay on our asses all day."

Alex laughed. "Nah, youngster, maybe I won't take him to the park so he can stay on your ass and keep you on the right path." He finished before going out the door.

THANKSGIVING EVE: NOVEMBER 2018

Evans was awakened from his nap by the sounds of shouting throughout the house. He got up, cracked his bedroom door, and listened.

"You said you had everything covered, James! Now we are in foreclosure! You said you were going to ask Wyatt for the money! We have maxed out our loans and cashed in Evans's college fund!" yelled Carmen.

"Just calm down, baby, I have a plan that will get us out of this for good. Just be patient with me. We have 90 days to come up with the money. Don't I come through all the time!" he responded, trying to keep Carmen calm.

Carmen took off her apron, grabbed her car keys, then exited the back door. When Evans heard the car start and leave the driveway, he withdrew from the bedroom and headed downstairs. He found his father sitting at the kitchen table turning a bottle of Jamerson up.

He looked up at his son. "Your mom is pissed off and left me with the cooking." He paused and began staring off into space.

Evans sighed and went over to the stove. He opened the oven and checked the ham before closing the oven door. He opened each pot on top of the stove, stirring the greens, moving the sweet potatoes around so they would not stick, and turning the turkey gravy on the warm setting. Afterwards, he joined his father at the kitchen table.

"Is there anything I can do to help? I overheard momma talking about the foreclosure, and I have been seeing the delinquent notices all over the place. Maybe I can get a job at the factory with Wyatt, or come to the dealership and help you out," suggested Evans, slowly taking the bottle from his father's hand.

James snapped out of his trance. "Son, give me your word that you will not tell your uncles about this. You understand me?" His words were slurring, but Evans understood.

"But, dad, you know they will help you and not think twice about it," Evans replied, hoping that repeating his mother's words did not invoke any consequences from his father.

"Look, son, as a man, and the oldest, you don't want to have your hand out. Don't worry, I have a plan. I may have to go to the dark side for a little while to get it. But I am sure it will work."

"Well, count me in! What's the plan? I want in!"

James looked at his son through drunken eyes. He hated accepting his invitation, but he needed him because he could not rely on anyone else to pull the plan off.

He snatched the bottle from Evans's hand and took a drink before breaking the plan down to his son. "Look, it's this warehouse in the west bottoms. I know some niggas on the eastside keep their stash there. I have been watching it for several months and I am confident of their schedule. They think they have everyone fooled, so they are laxed and don't check on the place much. We can go hit the place up in the next three weeks. I am sure based on the weekly drops that the stash is doing nothing but growing."

"Okay, dad, count me in. I will do whatever it takes to save our house and not go broke. But I will still ask Uncle Wyatt about getting me on at the factory for good measure." He took the bottle from his father and took a drink.

CHRISTMAS: DECEMBER 2018

"And the winner of the Walk It Out 2018: Strut Your Stuff winner is … Bella!" yelled the judge over the microphone before snapping his fingers.

Everyone cheered as Banks claimed his prize of $15,000. He had never had so much money at one time before. He could not wait to spend it and he planned to tell Adams and Evans. He would not be able to explain to his father or uncles where he won the money, because that meant he had to reveal that he was homosexual.

He hurried to the dressing room, transforming from Bella to Banks. Afterwards, he left the club and took a cab home. Once he arrived, Adams met him in the foyer with an alarmed look on his face.

"Where have you been? Shit has been going down all day," he whispered, taking Banks to his bedroom.

When they entered Adams room, Banks opened the bag and showed him the money.

"What the hell! Were you the one that broke into Uncle Wyatt and Uncle Alex's stash?" Adams muttered, locking the bedroom door.

Banks looked confused. "Stash? What are you talking about? Remember, I was practicing for the Strut Competition this year and I finally won! The prize was $15,000!" responded Banks with a proud look on his face.

Adams sighed in relief and responded, "Oh, yeah, I forgot about that! Congratulations. But let me fill you in. Someone hit up Uncle Wyatt and Uncle Alex's safe and $15,000 is not even an eighth of what is missing," he said, hiding the duffle bag of money in his closet. "Uncle Alex is on a war path. I have never seen him so mad before!"

"Damn, that's messed up! But you know the whole town been hating on him since he came up. There is no telling who could have broken into their place. Plus, Uncle Alex has been on some superman shit lately, it's rubbing people the wrong way," said Banks.

"How do you know that? You not in the streets and we both hear the same shit at the barbershop. So, what are you talking about?" Adams inquired.

"Look, I don't be in the streets, but I have street niggas for boyfriends. So, I hear a lot of stuff. You know that pillow talk is the devil and I get it all the time."

"Oh, so you a hoe? What happened to classy? I told you to stop fucking with all these niggas out here."

"Hey, boys! It's time to head over to your grandma's house!" yelled Duncan before heading downstairs and out the front door.

The boys exited the bedroom and went downstairs. Adams set the alarm, then they both headed to the driveway where Duncan waited in his Chevy Tahoe.

On the way to Rose's, Duncan warned his boys about Alex, "Be careful around Uncle Alex tonight. He is on the war path, some shit happened."

Fifteen minutes later, they parked in front of Rose's house and went inside. That night, Alex never showed up to his mother's house. He was busy hitting the streets, trying to find who had taken his money. Meanwhile, Wyatt took a different approach. Instead of wasting all his energy driving around, he would be humble and patient. He knew the information would surface eventually. Being a hustler, he was always prepared to take losses. The robbery had not broken him financially because he never kept all his money in one place. He invested a lot of his money, so it was growing both legal and illegally. However, Alex was different. He kept his money the old school way because he did not trust financial institutions, or anything being monitored by the government.

"Brother, I don't see how you could sit here so calm, and you just lost about 80k!" said Duncan, handing his brother a drink.

"Brother, money is not everything. I mean, don't get me wrong, it was a devastating hit, but not a blow. I am more concerned on who was able to get into the storage building like that and who is watching us that close. The security footage was destroyed, and it could take weeks if not months to recover that footage," said Wyatt, taking a drink of his Hennessey.

"You've been having that place for years and never had any issues. Only family knows where the spot is," said James, now entering the family room.

Evans entered shortly after, interrupting their conversation. "Hey, pops, can I take the escalade for a few hours? Banks, Adams, and I want to meet up with some friends and hang out."

Without saying a word, James tossed his son the keys. He watched him and his nephews exit the room on each other's heels. The boys hopped inside the Escalade, then Evans pulled out the driveway.

"What's been going on with you, Evans? We didn't see you for Thanksgiving," questioned Banks.

"Man, shit got rough. My pops was in debt. We were about to lose our house and everything. So, I spent Thanksgiving listening to him and my mother arguing. But we good now! We hit up this warehouse and came across the money to pay everything off. Problem solved," responded Evans, never taking his eye off the road.

Adams and Banks gave each other a suspicious look.

"You know that Uncle Alex and Uncle Wyatt's stash got hit up too. And I overheard that they didn't keep their stash at the loft, but at some secret warehouse that we don't know the location of," said Adams.

Everyone road in silence for several minutes before Evans spoke, "I don't think our robbery has anything to do with Uncle Wyatt and Uncle Alex. My father wouldn't back stab his brothers like that!" replied Evans, not confident in his statement.

"Shit, when you under the scope and about to lose it all, you never know what you would be pushed to do. Have you ever heard of a loyal snake?" questioned Adams, looking out the passenger back window.

"Here you go making up your own words," joked Banks.

"No, really, I read about it in this urban fiction novel called "Loyal Snakes". The author, Rosa James, lives in Kansas City, Missouri. She defines a loyal snake as a person that is obligated to be loyal to you because they are your family; but will stab you in the back. Stay woke. Times have changed and the need for money brings out the ugly in people," countered Adams.

"First of all, when did your ass start reading for leisure? And I don't see my father becoming a loyal snake," said Evans as he continued to drive.

MARTIN LUTER KING HOLIDAY: JANUARY 2019

It was a cold Monday night. Banks exited the drama club to find his Uncle Alex parked in front of the building. Confused, Banks approached the car, opened the passenger door, and got inside.

"Hey, Uncle Alex. What brings you to my neighborhood?" questioned Banks.

Alex disregarded the question and began to drive. They drove for several minutes until they arrive to a warehouse on the westside of town.

"Where are we?" Banks asked he observed his uncle getting out of the car.

Alex still did not respond. He gestured for Banks to get out and follow him. They walked past the warehouse and down by the river. Banks stopped in his tracks, not sure why his uncle was taking him by the river. When Alex noticed Banks was hesitant, he pulled his gun.

"Little nigga, walk your ass over by the water!" Alex demanded, snatching Banks by his collar, and pushing him ahead of him.

"Uncle Alex, what are you doing?" Banks asked, walking closer to the water.

Once they made it to the edge, Alex ordered Banks to hand over his backpack. When he opened it, there was the remainder of the money Banks won in the competition. When Banks noticed Alex looking at the money, it was clear that he thought it was from his stolen stash.

"Wait, Uncle Alex! That money is not your money, I won that," he pleaded.

But Alex didn't have any more words, he was sure that his nephew had been responsible for taking his money. He was sure that one of Banks lovers had convinced him to find the stash, and he was given a cut when the job was done.

Alex aimed and pulled the trigger, sending a shot into Banks's chest followed by one between his eyes. He watched his nephew fall into the water before he walked away, showing no emotion. Alex sat inside his car before driving to an apartment that he shared with his girlfriend, Janay and laid low for a couple days.

One Week Later

"Mr. White, we believe we have found Banks's body in the Missouri River," spoke the detective, sitting across from Duncan and Wyatt at the station.

"Nah, you haven't found my son. I need to see the body before I believe that shit!" responded Duncan, trying to hold back his tears.

They left the police station and got inside Wyatt's Lexus. They followed the police car to the Baton City morgue. When they exited the car, Duncan's legs felt like noodles. His heart pounded so loud, it sounded like a drum beating in his ears.

Wyatt felt his stomach doing flips as they followed the detective down the hall to a glass window. The room beyond the glass was empty at first, until the detective knocked on the glass three times. The staff rolled out a body covered with a white sheet. The detective gestured for the staff to remove the sheet, displaying the upper part of the body.

When Duncan saw Banks lying dead with a hole between his eyes and in his chest, he lost his breath. Wyatt was able to catch his brother, breaking his fall to the floor.

Wyatt looked up at the detective and uttered the words, "Yes, that's Banks White, my nephew, his son."

It took several minutes to get Duncan to the car. They left the morgue and headed to Rose's where everyone met up.

When they arrived, James and Alex were sitting in the living room. James stood up and helped Duncan to the couch while Rose went to the kitchen to get Duncan some water.

When Adams heard his father, he ran from the den, and hugged him. "Daddy, please tell me it's not Banks!"

Duncan looked in his son's eyes and confirmed that his twin brother was dead.

Alex stood up and made his way over to his brother. "Don't worry, brother, I am on the streets to find out what happened." He immediately left the house, James following behind.

Alex entered his Range Rover and started the engine. James barely got inside the passenger seat before he took off. They road in silence for several minutes. He could tell something was off about his brother for the past week and it was not just about his money.

When James looked back, he noticed something familiar in the back seat. It was the custom-made backpack he had given to Banks for his sixteenth birthday last year. When Alex noticed James staring at the backpack, he pulled over and looked at his brother before allowing the tears to fall from his eyes.

"Look, I lost control. Banks was responsible for stealing my money," said Alex, wiping his tears.

James could not believe what he was hearing. His caramel complexion was now pale as he stared at his brother huffing and puffing.

"Look in the backpack!" said Alex.

James grabbed the backpack and opened it, observing the money.

"Brother, this is not even close to the fraction of the money you are missing!" James barked, tossing the backpack in the backseat.

"Shit, I know! He had one of his gay lovers hit me up and he just took a portion of the money for the job," countered Alex, wiping his face.

James suddenly felt sick to his stomach because he was the one that had taken Wyatt and Alex's money. But based on how Alex was reacting, James did not want the next victims to be he nor his son.

"Gay lover! Brother, this is fucked up. But I have your back, you need someone in your corner. We are just going to keep this between us, and we have to get rid of the backpack," James ensured, putting his hand on his shoulder.

Goodbye Banks

Adams and Evans stood over Banks's freshly filled grave. Everyone had left the cemetery and headed to the repast at Rose's house, but the two boys stayed behind.

"Who could have done this?" questioned Adams, allowing the tears to fall from his face.

Evans tossed the white rose on the pile of dirt. "I think Uncle Alex did it!" He looked at Adams in the eyes. "I have been doing some investigating and Banks's body was found by the warehouse that me and my father went to. I thought it was just a coincidence, so I went back to the warehouse and saw Uncle Wyatt's car parked at the building a week ago to confirm. Adams, the building that me and my father robbed was our uncle's stash."

"So, Uncle James could have been involved in killing Banks also?" asked Adams, wiping his face.

"I investigated that too, but I don't think he was actually there. He has been working extra hours at the dealership. He and my mother have been doing a lot of honey mooning lately."

"Uncle Alex probably thought that it was some of the money from the stash. But that's still ruthless. How could you kill your own family for money!" said Adams now fueled with anger.

"Adams, our Uncle Alex and my father are the true definitions of your term 'Loyal Snakes' you were talking about."

"Well, I don't know how I am going to live with knowing my uncles caused my brother's death!" finished Adams, placing a rose on his mother's grave next to Banks.

Evans put his arm around his cousin. "Don't worry, I am not feeling this shit either. My father was disloyal, and Uncle Alex crossed the line by killing Banks. He killed a helpless teenager, and it was his nephew. My father had me assist him in robbing his own brothers. These actions stand for nothing they taught us. I say we be done with it all. Let us make my father and Alex pay, then we'll leave Killer City."

Adams looked at his cousin, his eyes menacing. "Then, we are on the same page. You handle your father, and I will handle Uncle Alex. My brother's keeper."

He reached out his hand and Evans met his hand. "No, my true brother's keeper," he repeated.

They walked away from Banks's grave to Evans's new 2019 Audi and left the cemetery, heading to the repast.

The Repast

At Rose's house, Alex and James stood in the driveway, talking.

"How are you holding up, brother?" asked James, passing Alex the blunt.

"I am the best that I could be in this situation. I just wish I could find out who else was involved because Banks didn't have all that money!" He took a hit of the blunt.

"Just leave it alone. The worst result has happened, our nephew is dead. What more retribution would be satisfying?" questioned James.

"I know but watching Duncan suffering hurts me. And Wyatt, he is too humble for me," replied Alex, passing the blunt back to his brother.

Their conversation was disturbed by Evans's car parking in the driveway. He and Adams exited the car and walked up to them.

James hugged his son and nephew. "How are you two holding up? I know this shit is hard."

Adams looked Alex in the eyes. "The best we could be during this time. I would just feel a lot better if I knew what happened to my brother. I think someone knew he had the money on him he won from the competition. It would have been around ten thousand, because we spend five of it just fucking off." He paused. "Did you two know that Banks lived a secret life? He was a part of the LGBT community, that's why he was always at the drama club. He also participated in walk competitions. He had finally won his favorite one, the 2018 Strut Competition held on Christmas. But I could not put that in his obituary because my father didn't know. It would add more stress to his life right now if he found out." Adams finished and walked away, leaving James and Alex speechless.

Evans continued to stand there with a matter of fact look on his face. It was evident that the information Adams had given the two men was mind blowing; and based on their reaction, they knew how and why Banks died. He walked away satisfied with his confirmation.

When Evans entered the house, he took off his peacoat and kissed his grandmother and mother. He washed his hands and joined Adams in the kitchen. He was making himself a plate of food.

He stood by him and whispered, "They for sure killed Banks. We are going to proceed with the plan." He grabbed a paper plate and began filling it with food.

Outside, Alex had a breakdown and James tried to console him.

"I fucking killed my family for no reason. I was sure that he had something to do with it!" said Alex, now on his knees.

"Is everything okay out here?" asked Wyatt, heading down the walkway to the driveway.

"He's fine. He's just having a moment about Banks," said James, helping Alex back to his feet.

Both Wyatt and James helped Alex into the house and took him to the den. Duncan sat there in a trance, holding a bottle of Jamerson.

"You see that guilt setting in?" whispered Evans to Adams as they sat at the dining room table, observing the men.

"Right. Now his conscious is weighing hard on him. He should have thought about that before taking my brother's life," Adams spat in a low voice.

"I can't look at this sick shit any longer. Let's go turn a couple of corners and make sure our plan is airtight," said Evans, standing from the table and heading to the kitchen.

Adams left his plate on the table and went to the den to his father. He kneeled in front of him. "Pops, don't worry. It's just you and me now. We are going to be okay. I'm going to go check on the shop, and will be back to take you home later," he finished before hugging him.

Adams stood to his feet and gave his Uncle Wyatt a hug. He exited the den and out the front door. Evans was already waiting outside with the car running. When he got into the car, he spoke, "Let's go to the northside. I have some homies that we can get some guns from. Good thing I didn't mess off the three thousand Banks gave me as a Christmas gift."

"Sounds like a plan," responded Evans as he put the car in gear and backed out of the driveway.

When James made it outside, Evans was halfway down the street. He stood on the sidewalk confused because Evans never left without telling him goodbye.

"The boys are not taking this well at all," said Wyatt, now standing next to James.

"I agree. Hey, any word on the footage from the warehouse?" James asked.

Wyatt found it odd that James was questioning the footage and not focused on the death of his nephew. He made a mental note. "Nothing yet. My guy said it's pretty bad and may not be salvageable. But at this point, who cares. I want to know what happened to Banks," responded Wyatt before going back into the house.

James took his cell phone out and dialed Evans's cell. It went straight to voicemail. He shook his head and went back inside the house. He joined his mother in the kitchen and started helping with the dishes.

"Mom, how are you feeling?" questioned James, picking up a dish out the sink and drying it.

Rose took a few moments before answering, "Something is off about everything. I feel some bad energy. I hate to say it's my boys that I am feeling it from. I just don't know which ones yet. And as for my deceased grandson, he was not living that type of life, so why would someone just shoot him like a dog and leave him floating in the damn river!" Rose pounded the counter and stood gazing out the kitchen window at her backyard.

She remembered that Banks helped her landscape the summer before. It brought tears to her eyes knowing that she would never have Banks to help her. But she knew that he was in a better place and was now rejoicing with his mother.

"Don't worry, mother, we will get justice." Were the only words James could offer.

Rose turned to him quickly and spoke in a monotone voice, "I hope whoever is responsible burns in hell!" She left, leaving James alone in the kitchen to finish the dishes.

Alex stood in the doorway, witnessing the conversation between his mother and older brother. It hurt him that his mother walked past him without saying a word. It felt like she knew that he had been the one that pulled the trigger. Alex could not find comfort in being around his family while they mourned for a loved one that he had taken with his own hands, so he decided to leave.

"Brother, I have to get out of here. I just cannot take it," said Alex before turning and heading to the foyer to grab his coat.

James hurried behind him, catching up before Alex made it out the front door. "Just make sure you answer my calls. I will come by the apartment and check on you before I go in for the night. It's on twenty fourth street, right?"

Alex nodded before going out the door. On the way home, he cried like a baby. Prison had changed him, and he did not know why he snapped. To make matters worse, he took an innocent life. He had to be honest with himself and admit that he never cared for Banks because of his sexuality. He wondered if those feelings toward his nephew made it easy to pull the trigger. Now, he had to live with the reality that he had killed Banks and caused so much pain to his family.

MEMORIAL DAY: MAY 2019

After months of observation and preparation, Adams and Evans were ready to make their move on Alex and James. Duncan opened the barbershop back up to the public. Wyatt continued to work at the warehouse and had plans on marrying his girlfriend, Denise, who was expecting his daughter.

Alex became more distant from his family. The guilt of killing his nephew weighed hard on him. He spent his days in seclusion drinking and snorting cocaine. Rose decided to sale the big house and move to Atlanta. After losing her grandson, she was done with Killer City.

James resumed life as if nothing happened. He was thriving at the dealership. However, the accomplishments had him stepping out on Carmen. She found out when his mistress showed up at their doorstep with a brand-new baby. Evans helped his father pack his belongings and move into a new apartment that was only a few blocks from Alex. But it was a waste of time because Carmen filed for a divorce and moved back down south to be with her family in Homestead, Florida.

It was 6:00 am when Wyatt was awakened by his alarm clock. He sat alongside his bed and looked back at his soon-to-be wife. She laid on her back, still sleeping peacefully, her pregnant stomach protruding through the comforter.

Wyatt smiled and softly rubbed her belly. "Good morning, baby girl. Finally, a girl in the family. I can't wait to meet you and spoil you."

Suddenly, he heard his phone vibrate. When he checked, it was a text message from Adams. He requested that everyone meet at the riverbank, say a prayer for his brother, and release some balloons for Memorial Day.

Wyatt confirmed before checking the other messages. He stopped when he seen the message he had been waiting on for months.

"Hey, this is Kylie. Please lock in my new cell number. I finally got that footage together, but I could only put it on a video tape. I hope you still have a VCR. I will meet you at Starbucks this afternoon."

"Thank you and okay," he responded before heading to the restroom.

As he showered, he thought about what he would find on the tape. Based on how the family had divided, he would not be surprised if it were someone close in his circle. He shook his head, wanting to ignore his assumptions and decided to wait on the facts.

He made plans to handle a few things at home before going to the flower shop to pick up some flowers. He planned to stop at the Wal-World to purchase some balloons and lanterns. He wanted to make things special for Adams. He was finally ready to go to the last place his brother was known to be alive. Suddenly, he remembered that he had a VCR at the warehouse near there, he would watch the tape after the ceremony.

At the apartment, Alex laid in bed and read the text message from Adams.

"Uncle Alex, I am ready to move forward from my twin's death. The only way I can do this is by going to the last place that he was alive. Could you please join me this evening? Please bring balloons. See you later."

He sighed after reading the text message. He didn't want to go back to the place because it would bring back the memories that haunted his dreams every night. He remembered the terrified looked in Banks's eyes when he pointed the gun to him. Now, knowing that it was genuine, made him feel sick to his stomach.

He grabbed the tray from the nightstand and took a line before going into the kitchen. Janay was frying eggs. He stood behind her and kissed her on the neck before patting her on the ass. He then went to the bathroom to shower. After getting dressed, he ate his eggs and rice and left some money on the table for Janay.

He could feel death on his back and learned to acknowledge his intuition. He knew his days were numbered and God's punishment would be death instead of prison this time. Before he made it to the door, Janay stopped him. When he turned, she handed him a pregnancy test with two lines, and smiled.

"Baby, you finally get to plant a seed on this earth."

He kneeled, matching her five-one height and kissed her lips. "I want you to do me a favor, baby. Take all the money out the safe and use some of it to go buy that house we were looking at the other day. I want you to never return to this apartment after today."

He left her in the doorway in silence. She began to cry because she knew that meant he was not coming home that night.

Adams entered his father's bedroom with a tray of his favorite breakfast, consisting of steak and eggs. He wanted to cheer his father up and show him that he appreciated him.

Duncan sat up in the bed and rubbed the sleep from his eyes. He smiled, seeing his son holding the tray of food. "Thanks, son. I remember Banks used to bring me breakfast every Monday morning before he asked me if he could go hang out at the drama club. I think he was trying to butter me up all this time." He laughed, using the knife and fork to cut his steak.

Adams sat on the bed and watched his father eat in peace. When he was almost done, he spoke, "Look, pops, I want to go to the place where Banks was last alive. I want you and all my uncles to be with me this evening so we can release some balloons. I feel this will help me move forward and begin healing." He finished and waited for his father to speak.

The thought of going down to the river made Duncan's stomach turn, but that didn't stop him from finishing his plate. He had not eaten much since Banks's death. Once the plate was clean, he took a drink of his orange juice, and looked at his son. Adams and Banks were identical twins, but they fought hard to look different, wearing different hair styles.

Banks wore his hair clean cut and trimmed neatly, letting it be known he was the son of a barber, while Adams preferred the messy hair look like his mother, who had worn her hair natural. But once Duncan returned to the barbershop, Adams had requested to have his hair cut exactly like his brother's. He knew that Adams was doing it to help him cope with losing Banks and he appreciated the gesture. Over the past few months, Adams stepped up and matured, no longer being that messy, defiant kid.

Duncan didn't want to let his son down, so he swallowed hard. "Yes, I will be honored to go pay tribute to Banks this evening. We should go get those lanterns I saw at the store the other day," finished Duncan, sitting the tray on the empty side of the bed.

"Okay, dad. I will go get ready. I already asked Uncle Alex and Wyatt. Evans is going to let Uncle

James know. I am so happy you are coming!" Adams exited the bedroom and headed to his room to call Evans. He answered on the first ring. "Everything is good on my end. Did you let your pops know?" questioned Adams.

"We all good over here, brother. I will see you later." Evans ended the call.

He went into his father's bedroom to find him asleep with one of his picks of the week. He stood over him and stared, not believing that his father was such a snake.

Feeling like someone was watching, James opened his eyes to find his son standing over him. "Is everything okay?" James questioned, tossing the sheet on the naked woman still asleep beside him.

"Adams has requested that we all go to the place where Banks died this evening. I was thinking that we could ride together," said Evans before leaving the room, not bothering to close the door behind him.

James started to say something, but instead, he got out of the bed and closed the bedroom door. He sighed and put his hands on his head because he did not want to go. He woke the woman in his bed up from her sound sleep.

"Can you get up and cook breakfast?" he questioned, expressing irritation in his voice.

The Celebration of Banks

Everyone pulled up at the warehouse at the same time. When they stepped out of their cars, each carried a bundle of blue, gold, and silver balloons along with lanterns and red roses. Everyone greeted each other using minimum words.

"The detective said they found him over there," said Wyatt, pointing over to an area of the riverbank.

He began walking towards the riverbank as everyone followed behind him. While walking, Adams noticed that Alex was leading the way, walking slightly ahead of Wyatt. The sight of it fueled him and he found it hard to keep from reaching for the gun in his waist. He wanted to blow his head off right then.

When they made it to the area where he was found, everyone stood in silence for several minutes looking around. Evans looked at Adams, giving him the cue to proceed, but was interrupted by Wyatt.

"After we say a prayer, then release the balloons and lanterns, I have something to show everyone inside the warehouse," he said.

His plan threw things a little off for Adams and Evans, who had originally planned to handle things on the very ground where Banks died. However, their curiosity kept them at bay.

"I can't believe my son is gone. I just feel so empty," said Duncan, still wiping the tears from his face.

Wyatt put his arm around his brother to console him. "Let it out, brother. This will help us all move on. Evans, can you lead us in prayer?" he requested.

Everyone bowed, Evans led the prayer, then, they released the balloons into the air.

"This is for you, son. I miss you so much," Duncan cried, lighting the lantern, and releasing it into the sky.

Wyatt lit a lantern and handed it to Adams. He walked up as close to the riverbank as possible and released it.

Alex stood quietly as he watched his brothers and nephews mourn the loss of a person whose life was taken by his hands. He felt sharp pains in his chest, feeling as if he could not breathe. He kneeled and released his lunch onto the ground. When he looked up, he noticed that Adams was standing in the very spot that Banks stood before he died. Now crying, Adams stood to his feet and Wyatt handed him a balloon.

Alex looked up at the sky, released the silver balloon, then spoke, "I will see you soon, nephew."

"You good, brother?" questioned Wyatt, patting him on his back.

Alex nodded and took a couple deep breathes to gather himself. For the next half hour, they stood sharing memories about Banks and consoling each other. He stood silently and listened as he had no good memories to share because he had been away. Now, he was just patiently waiting for his cue to leave.

Adams returned to the edge of the riverbank and looked out onto the murky water. He looked to the sky and admired the sunset, Evans joined him.

"We are still going to handle his shit here tonight," Evans ensured.

Adams nodded in agreement and tossed the red rose into the water.

"Hey, everyone, follow me," instructed Wyatt, now making his way towards the warehouse.

Alex fired up his blunt and followed Wyatt. James and Duncan dragged behind him. Adams and Evans allowed everyone to walk ahead before proceeding. When they were all in the warehouse, Wyatt led everyone upstairs to the secret security room and turned the power on.

Duncan could not stop crying. He took a seat along the wall in the room and buried his face in his hands.

"What do you have to show us?" James asked, growing worried.

Alex stood by Duncan waiting, he was hoping it was the information that Wyatt had been waiting for. Adams and Evans stood on opposite sides of the door, determined that only four people was leaving this room.

"God is good, my people. We were able to salvage the security footage so we can see who broke into the warehouse and stole our shit," said Wyatt, pressing play.

His words made James feel lightheaded. His heart pounded, wondering if the footage would be clear enough to reveal who robbed his brother's stash. He didn't have a gun on him to protect himself, but he was going to take the full responsibility to save his son.

Everyone stood in silence and watched two men breaking into the warehouse. Once they cleaned the safe, they both turned to the video camera, displaying familiar faces.

"What the fuck is this shit!" said Wyatt, turning around from the screen. He found Adams with a gun drawn on Alex, who never stopped looking at the monitor.

"What are you doing, son?" yelled Duncan, now standing to his feet.

Suddenly, Evans pulled his gun and pointed it at his father. "Father, how could you take me to rob our flesh and blood? We are supposed to be family! Why didn't you just ask them for the money? You know they would have given it to you with no questions!" he yelled with tears flowing from his eyes.

"What the fuck is this!" screamed Wyatt, shocked at what he witnessed from the video and what was unraveling before his eyes.

"Uncle Wyatt, play the footage from the night that Banks didn't come home!" demanded Adams, never taking his eyes off Alex.

Wyatt raveled through the menu as everyone stood in silence.

"Brother, I can't believe you," said Alex. He was now aiming his gun at James, who stood still while looking at his son.

"Uncle Alex, lay off that trigger until we watch this footage!" ordered Adams.

Alex never took his eyes from James. "No worries, nephew. It's all coming out tonight and you will get the retribution for your brother," he said. He then looked over at Evans. "Nephew, I am sorry your father did this to you. But you don't want his blood on your hands, trust me."

Wyatt found the footage from the night Banks was last seen alive. He fast forwarded it until he saw some activity. At 8:30 pm, Alex parked his car. Everyone watched quietly as Alex and Banks made their exit. The video shows Alex drawing his gun as he followed behind Banks. The footage was not able to view anything beyond twenty feet. However, you could hear two gunshots followed by Alex walking back to his car alone with Banks's backpack.

"You killed my son!" yelled Duncan as he punched Alex as hard as he could, causing him to stumble back almost dropping his gun.

When he regained his balance, he used his free hand to hold his jaw. "I'm sorry, little brother, I thought he took my money."

Duncan punched him again. "No, you killed my son because you thought he was gay! You were never bothered by any money!" he shouted.

"No, he didn't, pops. He really thought that Banks stole his money. But the truth is that Banks was a part of the LGBT community. He won $15,000.00 on Christmas from a competition. He could not tell you where he got the money from because that meant he had to reveal his sexuality to you. So, he kept the money a secret. But that didn't give this nigga an excuse to take my brother. We could have handled this another way!" shouted Adams, growing antsy.

"Be cool, Adams, you going to get your retribution. I take responsibility in the part I played in all of this. But not before we handle the root of it all," Alex stated, returning his focus to James.

"Come on, brothers. My nephew lost his life over money. Alex, I didn't care about that stash being hit up, money comes and goes!" spoke Wyatt, shaking his head.

"It's beyond money now, Wyatt. We can't leave here and move forward knowing what really happened!" Duncan said. He ordered Adams to give him the gun; but he refused and demanded his father to take a seat.

"Father, I can't believe you did this. You are the reason why Banks is dead. All because of your gambling, drinking, and cheating problems," said Evans in a calm voice.

"Son, for what it's worth, I was trying to make your mother happy," responded James.

Evans gripped his gun and prepared to pull the trigger, but before he could shoot, Alex took the shot, shooting James between the eyes. Everyone watched James body fall to the floor.

Alex then looked at Adams. "Handle your business now, nephew. I deserve it."

Suddenly, Duncan stood to his feet and pulled a gun out. "You are right, you do, my brother's keeper." He shot Alex in the neck, then the chest before hugging his son and taking the gun from his hands.

For the next half hour, everyone sat inside the room in silence as James's and Alex's bodies laid on the cold concrete floor.

"So, how do we explain this shit?" questioned Duncan, looking at his brother sitting at a desk with his hands covering his face.

"It's simple. They shot each other after viewing the footage," said Adams.

Everyone looked at each other in agreement. They set things up to appear that James and Alex shot each other.

After staging everything, they all left the warehouse. Before leaving, Wyatt tampered with some wires, causing a fire to start. Everyone went home and waited to be contacted by the authorities about the warehouse fire and the discovery of James's and Alex's bodies.

FATHERS DAY: JUNE 2019

Duncan sat in the NICU at Baton City medical center, holding his new-born niece. "Man, she a little early, but right on time. Finally, a girl in the family. I didn't think we was ever going to get one," he spoke, putting the binky back into her mouth.

"I can't believe I am a father now. Shit, you are going to have to have you another baby so my daughter can have someone to play with!" joked Wyatt.

Duncan laughed. "Nah, we twins, and I had the twin boys. So, it was your responsibility to have the twin girls. Besides, in a few more months, she will have her little cousin, Alexandria, to play with. And Uncle Duncan going to spoil them rotten and teach them to cut hair in my new shop."

They both started laughing before the nurse came into the room interrupting them.

"The mother has requested for us to bring Chanise to her room." She took the baby from Duncan and placed her in the basinet. She rolled her out of the room and down the hall.

Duncan stood up and took off the paper gown. "Let's walk down to the Entertainment District and enjoy some drinks and cigars. It's your first Father's Day, so let us do it like kings," he suggested, adjusting his Nike sweatsuit.

"Sounds like a plan. Let's stop by Denise's room and check on her before we head out. She still may want me to bring her something back," responded Wyatt, leaving the room.

After checking on Denise, Wyatt and Duncan walked down the hill to one of the bars. They took a balcony table to enjoy the warm June weather and view.

Duncan instructed the waitress to bring a couple of appetizers and a bottle of Cabernet.

"Red wine? You're classy now. When did you start drinking this, brother?" Wyatt kidded while Duncan poured them both a glass.

Duncan laughed and handed his brother one of the glasses. He held his up for a toast. "Boy, you a father now. This red wine is that grown man shit. Congratulations and happy Father's Day, brother!" he finished.

The brothers made their toast, enjoyed their appetizers and wine, then ordered their main course. After they finished their meal, Wyatt spoke, "Brother, do you still think about Memorial Day?"

Duncan looked around before responding, "Sure, I do! Hell, it wasn't that long ago, and I am still not getting much sleep. I can't believe how shit went down. And Banks was so innocent in the situation. Man, I wish he would have been comfortable with telling me the truth about his sexuality. I feel maybe that would have spared his life." He stopped, poured another glass of wine, then continued, "And our older brothers, I don't see where things went wrong with them. But bottom line, I no longer want to be here in Baton City. I am thankful that the shop sold so fast, and I found a space in Atlanta close to mom. I can't wait to get away from Killer City because there is nothing else left here for me."

Wyatt refilled his glass. "It was greed and pride, brother. You know money has a way of changing people. But on a better note, as soon as my transfer is approved for that manager position at the Atlanta assembly plant, and Denise and Chanise can travel, I am right behind you, brother. Janay already found a place in Florida close to Carmen, so there is nothing left here for us," he finished before drinking some wine.

San Diego, California

Evans and Adams relaxed on the balcony of their beach home. It was gifted to them from Wyatt who received it years ago from a settled debt.

Evans was set to start pursuing his law degree at The University of San Diego Law the following fall, while Adams pursued his dream of becoming a book and movie writer. Adams presented Banks's writings to a publishing company and now had a major deal to publish his brother's book of poems along with his own novels. Adams wanted to become the next Tyler Perry and was dedicated to achieving his goal.

To survive during their journey, they had the money left over from the rest of the stash Evans had taken from his father's safe. They invested in a dispensary to increase their income along with investments and support from both Wyatt and Duncan. In addition, Evans's mother gave him money from his father's insurance policy. After learning what really happened to Banks, Rose gave both Duncan and Adams what was left over from Alex's insurance policy so the boys would be financially stable.

"Did you call your pops and tell him happy Father's Day?" questioned Evans.

"Yeah, we talked this morning. Aunt Denise had the baby today. But how are you feeling? I know Uncle James has to be on your mind," responded Adams.

Evans focused on the ocean, admiring the view before answering his cousin. "I feel fucked up about what happened, but it was necessary. I never want anyone around me that will stab me in the back."

Adams looked at Evans. "My brother's keeper always." He put his fist out for Evans to pound it.

Evans met Adams's fist. "The true my brother's keeper."

THE END

STORY TWO

ENVY

TABLE OF CONTENTS

THE END

Nicole's bloody body was dragged from the car down to the edge of the swamp. She was left there to rot or become food for one of the wild animals lurking. She could hear the car door close and drive away. The car stopped and began backing up. The man got out of the passenger side and walked back over to her.

Nicole's vision was blurry, but she could see the silhouette of the man walking towards her with a gun in hand. Her heartbeat was like a drum in her ear. When the man reached her, he pointed the gun.

She managed to look up at her killer. The man she thought loved her and was supposed to take her away from it all looked down at her with disgust.

Nicole could not believe that the man towering over her bloody body had done nothing but showed her love, patience, and was a father figure to her two sons. Suddenly, she remembered her grandmother's words.

"Girl, you are not going to be happy until one of these men kill you."

Despite the disposition, her grandmother's words made Nicole laugh for a moment.

"I am glad to see you smile one more time before you die," said the man. His voice was therapeutic and offered her a moment of sanity. He fired twice before turning and walking casually back to the car. He was confident that she was dead.

Now unable to see out of one of her eyes, Nicole listened to the car drive away. Currently, there was nothing around her but dead silence as she laid wearing her wedding dress at the edge of a swamp in Louisiana. The cool air by the water gave her goose bumps as she laid shivering, now accepting the fact that she was dying. She began thinking about her sons Ray'Shawn Jr. and Kent Jr. It made her sad that they would have to grow up without a mother. At that moment, she realized that her actions were selfish, and she failed her children just like her mother did her.

Now drifting away, she prayed that God would forgive her. But deep down, she knew she would be spending eternity in hell for being responsible for so many deaths.

"I am so sorry babies. God, please look after my boys," she spoke before taking her last breath.

RIVALS: MARCH 2015

"You have to get out of here quick. Before my baby daddy finds you here, he will kill the both of us," said Layla.

Kent sat on the couch unbothered by her words and continued to roll a blunt. Layla paced back and forth around the small, trashy apartment. He could hear the footsteps coming up the hallway through the thin walls. Suddenly, the doorknob jiggled followed by three loud pounds on the door.

"Kent, this nigga is crazy! Please climb out the window or something," pleaded Layla.

Kent did not respond as he finished rolling his blunt. He found it humorous that she would even suggest him climbing out of a window to get away from another man. He had been waiting for this moment to face his rival for several years.

Kent looked over at the three-year-old little girl and smiled. He reached in his pocket, took out his wad of money, and peeled off two fifty-dollar bills and a twenty. He tossed the two fifty-dollar bills on the table and handed the little girl the twenty-dollar bill.

He stood up and looked down at Layla, his six-one slim frame towering over her before speaking, "Make sure you buy my stepdaughter some groceries, give her a bath, comb her hair, and clean this nasty ass apartment up." When he saw a gun on the top of the refrigerator, he walked over and grabbed it.

"Come on, Kent, put his gun back and go out the fire escape," begged Layla as he headed to the front door. But her words fell upon deaf ears as she watched Kent open the door.

Once the door was completely opened, the man on the other side reached for his gun, quickly realizing that Kent was holding it in his hand. They stood in silence staring at each other for several seconds, allowing their eyes to speak to each other.

Kent displayed a devious look while Layla's baby's father, Ray'Shawn, stood in the doorway furious. Their stare was broken by Ray'Anna calling for her daddy, happy to see him. She walked past Kent and handed the twenty-dollar bill to her father. He picked her up before entering the apartment. Kent took the opportunity to walk past Ray'Shawn and out the apartment. He casually walked down the hallway but made sure he kept eyes in the back of his head. He knew he had crossed a serious boundary, and if Ray'Shawn had a gun, he knew it would have been a shoot-out.

Inside the apartment, as soon as Ray'Shawn shut the front door, he checked out the window and observed Kent getting into the passenger side of a blue Tahoe truck before it sped off. He took a mental note of the truck as he kissed his daughter and slid the twenty-dollar bill in his pocket. He took his daughter inside her bedroom.

"Ray'Anna, play with the new toys daddy bought you. I am going to talk to mommy," he said before closing the bedroom door.

Layla was nervous as she moved around the living room now cleaning up. She made sure she took the money Kent left off the coffee table and placed inside her triple K bra. As soon as she looked up, Ray'Shawn met her with a smack in the face. Her body flew across the room before landing on the couch.

"Bitch, you had this nigga in here around my daughter and he took my gun?" Ray'Shawn spat, now standing over her. Furious, he blacked out and began punching her repeatedly.

After several minutes passed, it was his daughter's cries and the beating at the front door that brought him too. When he looked down at Layla, she was bleeding and swollen, he could hardly recognize her.

Suddenly, the front door flew open, and the police rushed inside with their guns drawn. Ray'Shawn was put in handcuffs and led out of the apartment. Layla was rushed to the hospital where she would spend the next three months healing.

Ray'Shawn was charged with assault and was sentenced to eighteen months in jail. With no parents, their daughter went to live with Ray'Shawn's Aunt Carmen and her husband, Mitchell.

NICOLE

"Nicole, just go in the motel room and act normal. You will be fine," said Tanisha, sitting in the driver seat of the Grand Prix.

In the passenger seat, Nicole looked at her aunt and rolled her eyes before taking in a line of coke. She took a few minutes to allow her high to take affect before speaking, "Why can't you do it?"

"Because this nigga knows you. Just go inside and act normal, it will be fine. We need this money. Shit, I am tired of sucking Mr. Calvin's old, shriveled up dick to pay the bills," said Tanisha, reaching over Nicole and opening the car door.

Nicole gave her a look of disgust before exiting the car and slamming the door. As she walked toward the motel, the cold March Midwest air stung her legs as she strutted up the sidewalk sporting Tanisha's Steve Madden heels. She threw an extra switch in her step, drawing attention from the cars passing by.

When she reached the motel, she frowned at the trash and homeless people hanging outside. She kept her head down to conceal her face as she made her way to the last room on the first level. She knocked on the door and looked around, noticing her aunt was now parked in the parking lot.

When the door opened, she was amazed to see the handsome man standing over her. He looked just like the pictures in his profile.

"Damn, Fabian, I wasn't worth the Marriott," said Nicole, walking past him, not bothering to greet him with a hug.

Fabian laughed and smacked her on the ass. "Damn, baby, this my hustle spot, it's the first of the month. You wanted to see me, and I was not leaving the money. So here we are."

Nicole adjusted her short leather skirt and took a seat on the bed. "Well, where the weed at?" She looked around the room at all the drugs and money sitting around.

Fabian laid down on the bed and rolled over behind Nicole. He reached around her displaying a *Backwoods* stuffed with weed.

"For you, my dear," he joked as he began rubbing on her thighs.

"Damn, you wore all this for me today? Shit, I need to take you out on the town and show out with you." He continued enjoying her soft skin and fresh scent.

Nicole began to feel nervous because he was moving faster than she anticipated. She was in no condition to have sex due to a recent abortion.

"I want to feel the weed, baby, before I feel you," Nicole whispered in a seductive voice.

Fabian gave her a sneaky smile and turned on the television. "Okay, you want to watch a movie and chill? You got it." He rummaged through his DVD collection and selected the movie *Paid in Full.*

They watched the movie while smoking until Nicole received the text she was waiting for. She texted Tanisha back giving her the room number and confirmed that it was just the two of them. After pressing send, she deleted the message and focused back on Fabian. She slid her hand in his sweats and pulled out his manhood. The sight of it made her mouth water and she wished she could sit on it after sucking it.

"I see you have met big daddy," said Fabian in a low seductive voice.

Nicole smiled before wrapping her lips around him and using her tongue to tickle his shaft. She moved up and down slowly while staring up at him.

"Yes, take it all in," whispered Fabian before closing his eyes and gripping Nicole's head, motioning it up and down.

Suddenly, the door opened, and three men walked inside. Fabian had his eyes closed in complete relaxation. Nicole was so wrapped up in what she was doing, that she didn't notice anyone else was in the room until she felt a tap on her shoulder. She gave Fabian one last stroke before taking her mouth off him and standing up.

"Damn, baby, why you stop?" questioned Fabian, opening his eyes. When he noticed the three men standing around the bed holding guns, he looked over at Nicole who stood against the wall. "Damn, Nicole, you set me up? Just think, I wasn't looking at you like the trash you really are. What a waste of a beautiful specimen," said Fabian, pulling his sweats over his still erect dick.

"Shit, nigga, you know these trick bitches ain't about shit," said one of the men before laughing.

Nicole shook her head. Fabian's words were like needles in her chest. She had built a relationship with him online for the past few months and he had finally let his guard down. Now hearing that he looked at her more than just a hoe to fuck made her regret setting him up. She wondered if he was the one that would have given her what she wanted. But now, it was too late. Even if he survived, she would be the last face he wanted to see.

Her thoughts were interrupted by the gunshots. She watched the men riddle Fabian with bullets. They took the drugs and money and left Fabian dead in the hotel room. She followed the men and got inside the minivan that waited.

Nicole looked out the back window to make sure her aunt was following behind. Once she spotted the car, she turned back quietly and continued watching the men pass weed back and forth to each other while talking about what just happened.

"Did you see that nigga trying to act hard," said one of the men.

"Fuck that nigga. Shit, baby girl, what are you doing later? I need you to suck me up like you were doing in that hotel room," said the man in the backseat.

Nicole didn't say anything, she just looked out the window until they arrived at a Wal-Mart parking lot. She exited and got inside the car with Tanisha. She had already received the money and was counting it when Nicole entered.

"Well, here is your share of the money. I deducted your rent and the abortion money," said Tanisha, tossing the six hundred-dollar bills onto Nicole's lap.

Nicole grabbed the money from her lap, put it inside her purse, and continued looking out the window. She was usually hype for a good set up, but this one had her heart heavy. She felt connected with Fabian in just the short time she spent with him. Another good man was gone because of haters that didn't know how to get it themselves.

Tonight, Nicole was going to tell her aunt that this would be her last time setting someone up. She was ready to settle down and start a family. The trap queen life was dangerous and did not have a happy ending. She did not want to be like Tanisha who had done so much dirt, she could barely show her face around the city. Nicole wondered if her aunt felt any remorse for all the deaths she caused.

KENT: JUNE 2015

Kent stood admiring his smooth, chocolate skin in the bathroom mirror. Suddenly, he was disturbed by his older sister, Angie, beating on the door.

"Hurry up, nigga, I have to get ready for this party," she yelled from the opposite side of the door.

"Why are you getting ready so early? Juneteenth not going to be cracking until it gets dark," responded Kent, looking out the small bathroom window at the people outside already hanging out.

As he continued to survey, he noticed the girl that would change his life. She sat on the park bench across the street. Her friends huddled around her chatting with each other and laughing.

Kent hurried out of the restroom, almost knocking Angie over. He went down the stairs and out the front door. Once he made it to the curb, he slowed down and began his cool walk across the parking lot until he reached the girls.

"Hello, ladies, I never seen you in this neck of the woods before," spoke Kent, never taking his eyes off the girl.

She returned the stare and blushed as she opened her sucker. She began sucking on it, giving Kent a seductive show.

"Now you remember all of us. My aunt threw that big party last summer," said one of the girls.

"Oh, yeah, Ms. Martha is cool peeps. She always looking out for everyone. I didn't know she had a niece. What's your name?"

"Her name is Simone, and my name is Nicole if you were wondering," said the girl sitting on the bench.

She stood up and walked over to Kent, taking his attention away from everyone else. Simone rolled her eyes and turned back to the rest of the girls. Kent seemed like a good catch, but she was used to Nicole hogging all the cute guys. It no longer bothered her.

"Well, Nicole is too common for a pretty girl like you. I think I am going to call you Treasure," said Kent, placing his hand on his chin, as if he was thinking, showing off his deep dimples.

Nicole rolled her eyes, but on the inside, the name Treasure gave her butterflies.

"So, will you be out later tonight? I would love to spend more time with you," questioned Kent.

"Oh, I will be wherever you are," responded Nicole, showing her white teeth.

"Okay, well, catch you later, Treasure," said Kent before heading down the street to catch up with one of his homeboys.

"Girl, do you know who that is?" asked Rochelle, one of Nicole's friends.

Nicole turned to her and shrugged, she didn't know anything about him, but she planned to learn more soon.

"That's Jarvis's older brother. They are coming up. I am sure they will be legends in the next few years," continued Rochelle.

"Damn, Rochelle, you stay on top of everybody," joked Nicole.

The three girls shared a laugh before returning their focus on the crap game that had started across the parking lot.

Later when the sun went down, everyone headed to the park to enjoy the Juneteenth event. There were live bands, vendors, and food trucks all over. While all the girls were preoccupied with catching a baller with a nice car, Nicole kept her eyes open for Kent.

Hours passed and she became frustrated. She couldn't believe she allowed him to get her excited only to stand her up. She grabbed Simone's tequila and took a couple shots. She refused to wallow in disappointment for a nigga that she barely even knew. As the night went along, she began to have fun and Kent was now at the back of her mind. She began flirting with some of the guys who had been pursuing her throughout the night.

"Hey, you want something to drink?" asked a male voice.

Nicole turned around, hoping it would be Kent. She was disappointed to find it was not. The man that stood before her looked older, but he was attractive with a sexy voice. Nicole smiled and nodded.

He took a fresh half pint of Hennessey out of his back pocket. "Here is an unopened bottle. You can have it, I have more in the trunk of my car," spoke the man.

Nicole smiled and took the bottle, wasting no time opening it and taking a couple gulps. At this point, she would just get plastered and wake up in someone's bedroom or hotel room. She had given up hope on Kent showing up that night.

She sat and talked to the man for a couple hours. She learned that he was twenty-eight which was seven years older than she was. His name was Mitchell, and he was born and raised in Atlanta. He currently lived on the far eastside of town and owned various commercial properties.

His conversation reminded her of Fabian. Despite the fact Mitchell was interesting, she still found herself thinking about Kent.

Once the festivities started wrapping up, Nicole took Mitchell's number. Afterwards, she and her friends headed back to Simone's aunt's place. When they returned to the block, Nicole almost lost her breath when she saw Kent shooting craps. She was happy to see him but mad that he did not show up hours before.

"There goes your boy," teased Simone as they approached the group of men.

Nicole rolled her eyes; she didn't want to seem like she cared about Kent.

"Damn, what's up with your friend, Simone?" questioned one of the men approaching Nicole. He began playing with her red braids while lusting over her smooth, milk skin and green eyes.

"Back up, homie, that's all me. Once we get rid of those dead ass braids," said Kent, now collecting his money from the ground. He walked over to Nicole and gave her a kiss on the cheek. "You want to go get something to eat? Let me take you to my favorite food spot around the corner. We can walk and talk."

Nicole nodded, but in the back of her mind she was offended about his comment about her braids. As they walked, she wondered if he had a car. She usually required her men to have cars, or they did not have a chance. She wasn't for sure if Kent owned one but didn't want to be quick to assume things, so she just went with the flow.

"Be safe and I will keep the door unlock for you!" yelled Simone, taking a seat by one of the guys.

"Don't worry, she good for the night," said Kent, wrapping his arms around Nicole and guiding her down the street.

When they made it to the food place, Nicole was concerned about all the people standing outside. She hoped that no one recognized her as Tanisha's niece. Once inside, Kent ordered their food and purchased another bottle of liquor before returning to the block. They spent the rest of the night sitting on the porch talking.

Nicole decided to listen. She learned that Kent was a year older than she and was the middle child of three children. He lived with his mother, older sister, and a younger brother. His father died when he was very young. He graduated from high school and had no plans on attending college. His mother was currently attending school to become a nurse, so he hustled and made money to help out. And finally, the golden question that had been burning in Nicole's mind, Kent had a car but hated to drive.

He made her feel happy and secure. She could see herself with him every single day. She wondered was this what loved really felt like. Just before sunrise, Kent invited her inside to his bedroom in the basement of the house. They watched comedy shows and finished the bottle of liquor before falling asleep.

THE TRAP: DECEMBER 2015

Nicole stood in the middle of her bedroom staring at the positive pregnancy test. She was happy, yet afraid of how Kent would react when he found out they had a baby on the way. She was thinking the worse, imagining him tossing her abortion money and never speaking to her again like she experienced in the past. Even though she was grown, she still felt like a little girl as she made her way down the hall to her aunt's bedroom. She entered to find her laying in the bed watching one of her favorite reality shows.

"Auntie, I have something to talk to you about," said Nicole, taking a seat at the foot of the king size bed.

Tanisha looked at her for a couple seconds before returning her eyes to the television and speaking, "Let me guess, you are pregnant."

Nicole sat looking at her, trying to figure out how her guess was dead on.

Before she could say anything, her auntie spoke again, "I could tell by the way you walked your scary ass in here. Your hips are spreading, and you have been spending too much time with that Kent nigga." She lit her joint and took a hit before continuing, "I know you are grown, but I am going to tell you this. Don't be stupid like your mother. She had a tendency of just attaching herself to men. Eventually, that shit drove her crazy and she now copes with drugs and alcohol. I have heard around town about this nigga. He is definitely street, and you know what comes with that, so just be safe."

Nicole turned away from her auntie and looked at the television. She hated how outspoken Tanisha could be. Now more than ever, she wanted to prove to everyone that she and Kent were going to make it. They would have a family and show everyone that they were meant to be. Nicole checked out of reality for several minutes and imagined her and Kent side by side. All the women would envy her, she would have everything a drug dealer wifey would want. He would buy her and their baby nothing but the best and everyone would respect her because she was the main woman.

The thoughts made her smile as she stared off into space. Tanisha sat disgusted witnessing her niece fall deeper into the pool of love for some nigga that she had only heard about on the streets. Not able to look any longer, she sat her weed down and clapped her hands, snapping Nicole out of her trance.

"Hey, you, get that lala land shit out of my bedroom," she demanded before returning her focus to the television.

"I don't see what's wrong with wanting more out of life. You know I want a family," responded Nicole, standing up from the bed and heading to the door to exit.

Tanisha turned from the television. "Well, let me tell you this. Niggas ain't shit, especially street niggas. The type of man you looking for won't have you for long. So why not set them up and get money? If you want a family man, you need to take your ass to church or mutha-fuckin IHOP," she finished, returning her focus to the television.

"*IHOP?* What does that have to do with anything? And that is why you are sitting here and cannot even enjoy life because someone might recognize you and blow your head off," Nicole fired back.

Tanisha sat up from the bed. "Bitch, how dare you judge me? Shit, the only reason why I am still in this raggedy town is because of you and my crackhead sister. Remember someone had to look after you while my sister checked in and out. I did what I had to do. Don't worry, as soon as you get out this bitch, I'm leaving Kansas City forever."

Nicole rolled her eyes and went into her bedroom. She dressed and grabbed her purse to head down to Kent's house. She wanted to give him the news in person.

Hours later, Kent's cell vibrated as he laid in Simone's bed trying to enjoy the head that she was giving him. He looked and observed several missed calls from Nicole. She had been calling him for the past three hours. He sat the phone down and continued his focus back to Simone who was a beginner at giving head. He was determined to make her a sex machine because he saw her potential.

"Simone, be consistent with your tongue motions, give the tip attention, and gag more," he instructed, staring at the ceiling.

Suddenly, his phone vibrated again. He snatched the phone up ready to curse Nicole out, but it was Angie. "What's up, sis?" answered Kent.

"Nicole is here at the house. She has been sitting here for about an hour. You need to get here, she has some news that you may want to hear in person," said Angie, looking over at Nicole who was sitting on the couch patiently.

"Okay, I am on my way," said Kent, ending the call. He pushed Simone's head from his dick. "I have to head out, and you need to watch more porn." He directed, pulling up his sweats.

He headed out the bedroom and down the stairs to the living room area where Ms. Martha sat on the couch. She was smoking a cigarette listening to her music. Kent tossed a gram of coke in her lap and exited the apartment without saying a word.

Ms. Martha rolled her eyes. "Well, good day to you too." She then looked up at Simone. She was now standing at the foot of the stairs. "I see you still don't got it right yet. That nigga's legs should be like noodles every time you touch him. You better get that shit together or you going to lose a nigga like that," she warned, returning to her music.

Simone rolled her eyes and headed to the kitchen to grab something to drink. Her aunt was right. She had told her everything to do to get Kent's attention and now she had to figure out how to keep him in her corner.

Outside, Kent hurried through the back alleyway to his house. Angie stood in the doorway waiting for him shaking her head. When he walked in the door and saw Nicole, he took a seat on the chair. He looked back and forth at his sister and Nicole, waiting for one of them to explain what was going on.

"Go ahead, Nicole, it will be better coming from you," said Angie, taking a seat next to her.

Nicole could feel her stomach turning. She felt like her breakfast would come up at that moment. Angie handed her the bottled water that was on the table. She instructed her to take a breath and just let it out. Kent sat in anticipation. He knew it could only be two things: pregnancy or a sexually transmitted disease. If he had to choose, he hoped it was a std that was curable.

When the words, "I'm pregnant." came from Nicole's mouth, his face felt numb and his stomach was in knots. Kent liked her but he was only twenty-two and was not ready for a baby nor a relationship. He had plans one day to have a family and he wanted his children to have both of their parents. His mother had raised him the best she could without a father, and he knew how painful that was.

Kent could tell by the way Nicole looked at him and searched for his response that she had no plans on getting an abortion. After taking his older sister to the planned parenthood, he never wanted a woman to go through that. He also knew his mother was not fully against abortion but had made the decision when she was pregnant not to abort any of her three children. He remembered her explaining that she could not live with knowing she had intentionally killed her child. She explained to her son that if God didn't mean for a child to be here, then miscarriage was natures ways.

"Kent, are you okay? Say something," said Angie, now standing over him with her arms folded.

Kent looked at Nicole and began to speak, "Treasure, I am going to keep it real. I didn't really want a baby this early in life, but I am not going to allow any of my seeds to grow up without me."

Nicole smiled, that was all she needed to know. She was going to have this baby, be a family, and prove her aunt wrong. Angie looked at her brother. She could tell he didn't want this, but she also knew that he was not going to make Nicole do anything that she didn't want to do with her body. She patted him on the back before exiting the living room, leaving the two alone to figure things out.

"So, what do we do now?" questioned Nicole with hopes he would now want to commit to a relationship and get a place together.

Kent didn't respond quickly; he was thinking about how he was going to break the news to his mother. He knew she was going to curse him out about his reckless behavior, but he also knew she had his back.

He opened his mouth and spoke, "Well, we just going to do what we have to do and get ready for a baby."

Nicole sighed in relief. She was glad that Kent did not hand her the abortion money and kick her out.

Suddenly, Jarvis submerged from the basement. He had been listening to everything and felt like now was the time for him to try and talk some sense into his older brother.

"Hey, bro, can I have a word with you outside," said Jarvis, not paying any mind to Nicole.

Kent nodded and looked over at Nicole. She sat on the couch looking tired and uncomfortable. He knew his brother was not fond of her but that no longer mattered now that she was carrying his child.

"Hey, why don't you go lay down in my bed and rest. I will grab your favorite from Top Spot and be back in a few," instructed Kent before exiting the front door.

Nicole smiled, went downstairs, and laid in the bed. She grabbed the television remote from under the pillow and flipped the channel until she found something to watch. She was now in the position she wanted to be in. She watched television until she dozed off.

Jarvis and Kent walked in the cold while passing a pint of Hennessy back and forth to each other.

"Look, bro, Nicole has been all through the town from hood to hood. Now I know people change but this chick plays the victim type. Years ago, I watched her let some niggas run a train on her and then she called rape. On top of that, she is Tanisha's niece. You know the set-up chick that has a bounty on her head," said Jarvis before taking a drink of the bottle. He passed it back to his brother before continuing,

"Trust me, she is the worst type of bitch. She thinks she can get by with just her looks and will set a nigga up. Plus, this isn't the first time she has been pregnant if you ask me, she is looking for a come up. Her mother is that Regina chick that be sucking dick for crumbs in the building a couple blocks over."

Kent gave his brother a questioning look. "You are talking about three-minute Regina?" He stopped in his tracks waiting for Jarvis's response.

When his brother nodded, Kent placed his hands on his head. He now remembered a conversation he heard his homies talking about Regina's daughter. She was getting down with whatever in abandoned buildings. She was even behind setting up a couple dudes they grew up with.

"Damn, that explains why she is a freak in the bedroom," mumbled Kent as he continued walking.

"So, what are you going to do? I say give her the money to go get an abortion and get the fuck out of this. You know we have plans to climb to the top and we don't need no bitch like that," suggested Jarvis.

Kent looked at his brother. "Nah, you know how I feel about abortions. Momma's story had me fucked up and I never want a woman to feel that way."

"But we not talking about our momma, we are talking about a hoe," countered Jarvis, finishing the pint. "Look, I look forward to being an uncle, but I just don't think you are making a good choice with Nicole. Remember what momma said, you lay down with the dog you catch the fleas."

They both laughed and continued walking and talking until they saw some of their friends. After chatting for several minutes, they went to Top Spot and ordered an Italian steak sandwich and a strawberry mixed with chocolate shake. They then went home, and Kent gave Nicole the food before leaving her again.

Kent wasn't ready to discuss things with Nicole yet. He knew he would be critical about her newfound history. The liquor had him in his feelings. He had to admit he was only physically attracted to her, and now she was pregnant. He felt trapped but still had enough respect for her not to force her to have an abortion.

He decided to go back over to Simone's to clear his mind and tell her what was going on. They had become friends with benefits, and he liked being around her. When he told her about the pregnancy, she seemed to take the news like a soldier. When they had sex that night, her performance had improved.

After chilling with Simone and Martha, Kent swallowed his pride and headed back home. He was going to try and make things work for the sake of his unborn child. But in the back of his mind, he hoped that mother nature would maybe see that he nor Nicole were ready to be parents.

Time passed and Kent's mother got over the fact that he had a baby on the way. Nicole moved from her aunt's house and with a little convincing, she was able to move in with Kent and his family until she was able to get her own place.

During that time, Nicole learned a lot about Kent's family and established a bond with them. Kent's mother was very attentive of her during the pregnancy and made sure she was living healthy. Angie took her to her doctor appointments. Jarvis kept his feelings to himself and supported his brother the best way he could in the situation.

But over time, Kent seemed to be more distant. He would come home every night but left bright and early every day. He only went to one doctor's appointment to find out the gender of the baby.

Nicole learned that Kent was a hustler, but he did not make the money that could buy her a car, house, and pay her bills. He was still trying to build something and get to that point, and she was willing to start at the bottom with him which would solidify their bond. She helped him bag his drugs and count his money and was willing to do anything that would help him get them rich and out his mom's house.

When their baby boy was born in August 2016, Nicole found out that Kent was a cheater. To make matters worse, he was cheating with her friend Simone which explained why Simone stopped talking to her when she told her she was pregnant.

Angie was good friends with Simone but stood by Nicole. However, once Nicole found her own place, she would be on her own and have to deal with Kent who had no plans in changing.

When the baby was two months, one of Kent's side chicks found Nicole's address and came to her house and beat her up. When Kent found out, he dealt with the girl and apologized to Nicole. But that didn't stop him from cheating and living the fast life. Having a son made him hit the streets harder, hustling more and that created more enemies along the way. His homies would hang out at Nicole's apartment smoking weed and playing the video game all day and night.

Nicole confronted Kent about the heavy traffic and noise which was putting her at risk of eviction. His response was that he was trying to get money and the apartment was not going to be where they were going to live so what difference did it make. She took his word and stayed in the bedroom. She would spend her days dreaming of what area of town she wanted to move to and what type of house she wanted.

Nicole wanted more children with Kent. The thoughts helped her to isolate herself and ignore all the different girls he was messing with. She convinced herself it was a part of the game and that she had to sacrifice to win at the end.

But as time passed, she began to give up hope. Kent was growing more distant and not the same charming man she met. She began to question if it was all worth it. Now her aunt's words were making a lot more sense.

RAY'SHAWN: DECEMBER 2016

Ray'Shawn walked out the side door of the Jackson County Correctional Facility. He thought no one was waiting, but relaxed when he heard his Aunt Carmen's voice calling him from down the hill. When he turned, his aunt was there along with his daughter, Ray'Anna. She stood next to Carmen pointing in the direction of her daddy. He hurried down the hill, being careful not to slip on ice. He hurried over, picked up Ray'Anna, and began hugging and kissing her.

After the brutal beating, Layla did not want to be connected to Ray'Shawn in any way, so she abandoned her daughter. Ray'Shawn vowed to stay with his daughter and never let any man hurt her like he had done her mother.

"Where's Uncle Mitchell?" Ray'Shawn questioned while securing his daughter in the seatbelt in the back seat of the car.

Carmen laughed before answering, "Boy, now you know that nigga is not coming near a jail. He is waiting on you to celebrate." She waited on Ray'Shawn to get inside before starting the car and driving away.

Ray'Shawn was glad to be out of the filthy county jail breathing fresh air. He ended up doing more than eighteen months because he had a couple fights and past warrants that came back to bite. He was fortunate that Kent had taken the gun from the apartment because the police searched it. If they would have found it, he would have to do more time. In jail, he had taken the time to think about what happened that day and vowed to get revenge on Kent.

They had always been rivals. Ray'Shawn was a blood and Kent was a crip. They respected each other's territories but if they encountered each other at parties, it was funk on sight.

In Ray'Shawn's eyes, Kent had crossed the line when he started hanging out in his hood and fucked Layla. By the time Ray'Shawn found out about the affair, his daughter was born. There were questions on whether she belonged to him or not. But when Ray'Anna entered the world, there was no doubt that the chubby, caramel little girl with big pretty curls belonged to him. Just as an extra measure, he paid for a DNA test because he watched Maury and the kids sometimes looked like the man that was not the father. Once he got the results back, he no longer had to question, and he and Layla made a promise to each other that they were going to leave the past behind.

But Ray'Shawn could not let go of his typical ways. He continued to cheat, and that made Layla go back to her ways of creeping. She could not resist Kent and as soon as she got the chance, he was right back between her legs as if they had never stopped.

Kent never cared about Layla, he just did it to get under Ray'Shawn's skin. Despite him having her eating out of the palm of his hands, Kent could never see himself with Layla because he wanted all his children to belong to the same mother.

Ray'Shawn was going to take any opportunity to catch Kent slipping and get him back at his own game. He had heard while locked up that Kent and Nicole had a baby. Ray'Shawn knew it would be easy to get back at Kent because Nicole used to let his homies run trains on her. He would get in with her and use her and Kent's son as a pawn in his game.

"Boy, what are you over there smiling about?" questioned Carmen.

"Just thinking about the first chicken head female I am going to hook up with tonight," he responded.

"Daddy, will the chicken be fried or grilled? Because I love Uncle Mitchell's grilled chicken," questioned Ray'Anna in the back seat, looking up from her iPad.

"I'm not talking about that chicken, baby, and stay out of grown folk conversation," joked Ray'Shawn.

Both he and Carmen laughed when Ray'Anna shrugged and returned to her iPad.

Later that night, Jarvis parked in front of Nicole's apartment and popped his trunk before honking the horn twice. Moments later, Kent came out with two trash bags of clothing and his Play Station. He went back to retrieve his boxes of shoes. When he went back inside, Nicole stood in the living room with her arms folded. Kent said nothing as he grabbed the hamper containing the box of shoes and exited the front door, leaving it wide open.

Nicole stood in the door and watched him load the rest of his things before getting inside the passenger seat. When Jarvis drove away, she slammed the door. She returned to her bedroom and sat down on the bed. She cried, finally fed up with Kent's cheating and broken promises.

Although her feelings were raw, it would be easy for her to try and move forward because she had been talking to Mitchell who she reconnected with. He convinced her to kick Kent out and move on. Nicole was not really into Mitchell, but he was a good distraction and put her up on a lot of game. At this point in her life, Kent no longer served the purpose she thought he would.

He was hustling but was not progressing and his legal issues kept his pockets light. After a while, it became hard for her to get him to buy milk for the baby or pampers. Once Kent started telling her to get a job, she really knew it was time to let him go.

"Girl, it is about time you let that nigga go," said Rochelle, rolling up some weed as she sat in the non-furnished living room.

"You're right. I can't believe I put all my hope into Kent. At first, it seemed like he was going in the right direction. Then he hit a couple legal issues and boom, couldn't even buy me the furniture he promised," said Nicole, taking a seat on the floor next to Rochelle.

"Don't worry about that shit anymore. There is this party tonight for my cousin that just got out. See if Angie can watch Kent Jr. so you can get out and enjoy yourself for a change," said Rochelle, passing the weed to Nicole.

Nicole smiled before taking a hit of the weed; she was more than ready to get back to her hoe days and forget about Kent. With revenge in her heart, Nicole was going to make sure that Kent would hurt just as much as she did by any means.

At Carmen's, Mitchell and Ray'Shawn relaxed in the mancave enjoying a blunt and drink.

"So, what's been going on with you, nephew?" asked Mitchell.

Ray'Shawn looked around admiring the scenery. This was what he wanted to live like, and he was going to make it happen.

"I'm good, Uncle Mitchell, trying to be like you and Aunt Carmen," responded Ray'Shawn. He took a drink of his scotch. "So how did those funds work out that I left before I went in?"

Mitchell smiled at his nephew; he couldn't wait to give him the good news. Ray'Shawn had given his stash to his uncle to flip right before he went to jail, and it paid off.

Mitchell and his homeboy Johnson flipped the money and now everyone was sitting fat. When Ray'Shawn went in, they had just begun. But they made sure to put Ray'Shawn's stash into the investment to grow his money.

"You good, nephew. I have an even bigger surprise for you and your daughter," said Mitchell, grabbing his keys. He finished his drink before gesturing for Ray'Shawn to follow him.

Ray'Shawn followed his uncle outside. They got inside Mitchell's red 1957 cutlass and took off. They drove for ten minutes before parking in front of a house not far from the subdivision where Mitchell and Carmen lived.

"Damn, this is a nice house," said Ray'Shawn as he exited the car. He followed Mitchell up the cobblestone walkway.

Mitchell used his key to open the door and enter. When he flicked on the light, Ray'Shawn was amazed.

"Man, Uncle E, I love what you been doing with these houses, damn." He walked into the foyer, then into the living area.

Mitchell answered, "Nah, when we flip houses, we just do what it takes to make it presentable for sale. But when it's family, we make sure it's the best of the best." Mitchell handed Ray'Shawn the house key.

Ray'Shawn gave his uncle a suspicious look, still holding his hand open with the house key inside. Was his uncle saying what he thought he was saying? Was this his house?

Suddenly, everyone jumped out and yelled, "Surprise! Welcome home!" Including his daughter.

Ray'Shawn damn near cried as he looked around at his family and friends. His Aunt Carmen gave him a hug before giving him a tour of his new home. It had four bedrooms. The master bedroom had its own personal bathroom and walk-in closet. The other bedrooms had their own personal bathrooms, and the basement was finished. It had a screened in patio and a stone exterior. The house was almost exact to the dream home Ray'Shawn had shared with his Aunt Carmen when they used to watch HGTV together.

The bedrooms were already furnished with beds. His daughter's bedroom was decorated with the best. He could do nothing but smile in amazement. It felt good having family look out for him when he was down. Ray'Shawn went into the kitchen and grabbed the bottle of Hennessy and opened it while Carmen went to the cabinet and grabbed shot glasses. He, his aunt, and uncle stood around the island and took a shot.

"Welcome home," they said in unison.

At Jarvis's downtown loft, Kent looked out the window admiring the downtown view. He was disappointed that he had allowed Nicole to take him off track. His little brother was right from the beginning. What made him change was when he got locked up for a month. During that time, she treated him like shit, always arguing with him about money during the calls. To make her happy, he sold his car to pay the lawyer and purchase the furniture that she nagged about but never bought.

"Bro, you don't need a bitch like that. I told you she was going to trip," said Jarvis, sautéing the steak in the skillet. When Kent did not respond he continued, "Look, don't worry, you didn't lose it all. I have been looking out for you and waiting for you to come out of that pussy coma." Joked Jarvis, placing the T-bone steaks on plates.

Jarvis placed both plates on the table, retrieved the salad, then a bottle of red wine from the mini cellar.

When he took a seat at the table, Kent smirked at his younger brother. He knew that Jarvis always liked the finer things in life because he would watch all the hood movies like *New Jack City*. Fact is, Jarvis would always say he was going to make money and live like a boss and not a hustler. Now, looking around his luxury loft, Kent was proud of his little brother for never losing sight of his dreams.

Kent dug into the T-bone steak and savored the flavor; his little brother would always be in the kitchen with his mother cooking, and it showed.

Jarvis ate half of his meal before pouring his brother a glass of wine and refilling his own. "Look, I have been looking out for you like I said before. Remember that money that those niggas robbed you of months ago? Well, you know I got that shit back and that nigga James made the ten o'clock news for it," said Jarvis, taking a drink of his wine. "I flipped that shit and you have a little something to get you back on your feet. I need a partner by my side while I deal with some out-of-town shit with my new connect. It would be an honor to have my brother with me."

"Hell, yeah, bro, you can count on me," responded Kent, finishing his food.

The brothers finished their meals and discussed the new business at hand. They were set to fly out to California in the morning, so Kent called his sister to make sure someone would check on his son while he was away. Angie was now married and lived up north with her husband, Adam, and was expecting a child soon.

Things had changed over the past few months. Their mother graduated from nursing school and moved out the neighborhood. She lived around the way from Angie.

No longer having the risk of jeopardizing his mother's home, Jarvis was able to hustle harder. While Kent was lovesick with Nicole, Jarvis was initiating the master plan to capitalize and be the king of the city. He patiently waited for his brother to come around so that he could share the throne. With no legal issues on his shoulders, Kent was ready to take his life to the next level.

Kent helped Jarvis clean up the kitchen after the meal and declined the invite to the strip club. He just wanted to chill, smoke, enjoy the view and some good company. With a new financial endeavor ahead, he was humble. Kent was proud of his brother and regretted falling off the track being wrapped up in Nicole. He never wanted to be down again and would earn his spot- on top of the food chain.

He sat in the dark and smoked his weed while admiring the downtown view. It had been months since he had felt so peaceful. He looked at his cell, noticing a text from Simone. She had become a good support system and friend during his troubles. She never turned her back on him and always gave him encouragement. He dialed her number and invited her over to chill with him for the night.

At Ray'Shawn's house, Rochelle found a parking spot in front of the beautiful house and turned the engine off. She looked over at Nicole who was fixing her make up in the overhead mirror. Once Nicole was finished, they exited the car and made their way up the walkway and into the house. When they walked in, everyone was smoking, drinking, and dancing. They went into the kitchen where there were endless bottles of various liquors on the island. They grabbed one of the red cups and made themselves drinks before joining the crowd.

Ray'Shawn stood in the corner of the living room observing everyone when he noticed Nicole and his cousin Rochelle exiting the kitchen. When Rochelle noticed him, she made her way over.

"Hey, cousin, I am so happy you are out. This place is nice," said Rochelle, hugging Ray'Shawn.

He embraced his cousin, never taking his eyes from Nicole. She stood patiently waiting.

"And look at little Nicole looking stunning as usual," said Ray'Shawn.

Nicole took a moment to give Ray'Shawn a once over. In her eyes, appearance was everything. His hair was cut low, displaying his fresh waves. His eyes were dark, and his face was freshly shaved. His smooth, caramel skin didn't have a scratch and when he smiled, his diamond grill shined. Nicole didn't care for gold and diamond grills. She preferred white teeth like Kent's. He didn't believe in wearing any type of bling but a chain and maybe a ring.

Nicole could not believe that despite her moving on, she was still comparing men to Kent as if he was someone. She shook her thoughts and focused back to Ray'Shawn who appeared to be on top now and digging her. She thought about how this could be a good way to get back at Kent and show him what he was missing. She knew that they were rivals. What would get Kent's attention more than Ray'Shawn flaunting her around town, showing him how she should have been treated in the first place.

Nicole hung close to Ray'Shawn throughout the night and when the party was wrapping up, she and

Rochelle hung out afterwards until the wee hours of the morning. Ray'Shawn ordered breakfast and the girls helped him clean his place up. Afterward, they sat and smoked, reminiscing about the days they used to have fun back in the fifties.

Nicole was supposed to meet Angie at 8:00 am at her place to get Kent Jr., but she didn't want to leave until Ray'Shawn put her out. She texted Angie and lied to her, saying that they went to St. Louis and got stranded and should be back by Sunday night. That would give Nicole the weekend to see what Ray'Shawn was really trying to do.

Ray'Shawn was satisfied now that he could put his plan into motion. He would get into Nicole's head and once finished, throw her back to her baby daddy. He reached in his pocket and pulled out the wrinkled up twenty-dollar bill that Kent had given his daughter. He would return the money to the owner or maybe even his son. It would be his signature once he was finished executing his plan.

ENVY: MAY 2017

Ray'Shawn parked his red jeep in front of the Sprint Center and got out. He strutted over to the passenger door and opened it. Nicole stepped out wearing a red dress, with matching hills and a tote. She looked around admiring all her haters that were staring. Ray'Shawn closed the door and they walked into the Sprint Center to take their seats for the comedy show.

Nicole turned around to gain one last look at her haters before entering. She lost her breath when Kent stepped out of his blue Camaro. She watched as her ex-friend Simone let herself out of the passenger seat wearing a blue dress that showed off her curvy hips.

Nicole rolled her eyes, grabbed Ray'Shawn's hand, and entered the building. After going through the metal detectors, she and Ray'Shawn found their floor seats. Nicole sat down and tried to be discreet as she looked around for Kent and Simone. She needed for him to see her happy and moving on with someone else. Her wish was granted when Kent and Simone walked in. Several minutes later, they came in and took their seats on the opposite side of the front row.

Ray'Shawn noticed Kent as well and hoped he saw him flaunting Nicole. He flagged the waitress over and ordered himself a Hennessey on the rocks and Nicole a ginger ale and nachos with extra peppers. She was five months pregnant with his son.

"You see your girl and her man trying to get your attention," whispered Simone after taking her vodka and cranberry juice from the waitress.

Kent grabbed his Hennessy and they both laughed. Then the lights went dim, and the comedy show began.

During the show, Nicole and Ray'Shawn were so preoccupied with getting Kent's attention that they could not focus on the show. Meanwhile, Kent and Simone enjoyed the show and each other as if nothing else mattered.

When the show was over, everyone exited the Sprint Center and hung out downtown. When Kent and Nicole finally made eye contact, he smiled before returning his focus to Simone. Ray'Shawn observed the transaction between the two and was disappointed that Kent was not showing any emotion about the situation. Not able to gain a reaction, Ray'Shawn gave up. He went to the valet and requested his Jeep so he and Nicole could go home.

Not wanting to end the night so soon, Kent and Simone hung out downtown before they finished their night at a hotel. Kent was happy that he was in a good place. He was grateful to be able to celebrate his achievements with Simone who had been holding him down and was good company.

Now at home, Nicole was irritated. She hated to see Kent wining and dining another woman because it was supposed to be her.

Angie had been taking care of Kent Jr. for months while she played house with Ray'Shawn. But now, it was time to use her son as a pawn to get Kent's attention. She laid in bed thinking of ways to get back at Kent until early the next morning. She slid out of the bed, being careful not to wake Ray'Shawn and went downstairs to the kitchen to call Angie.

When Angie answered, Nicole asked her to bring Kent Jr. to her apartment and she would meet her there. When she returned to Ray'Shawn's, he was just waking up. When Nicole came into the door with Kent Jr., the sight of the little boy agitated him. However, he kept his composure and focused on the bigger picture of getting under Kent's skin.

For the next few months, they played house with their blended family. They were taking pictures and posting them to social media talking about how happy they were with each other and their plans to get married. Ray'Shawn had not even proposed. They worked hard until they soon gained Kent's attention when Nicole start refusing to allow Kent Jr. to see his father or family.

Nicole's mother hated Ray'Shawn just as much as Kent because she knew him from the streets. She knew that he had a history of abuse, knowing it was only a matter of time before her daughter would become a victim. But she tried not to say anything to set her off since she was allowing her to stay at her apartment.

When Nicole gave birth to Ray'Shawn Jr., they continued to deceive everyone portraying as one big happy family. Nicole continued to ignore any calls from Angie and Kent in attempts to get Kent Jr. for visits. Her mother continued to keep a communication line open with Kent, giving him the scoop of what was really going on in the perfect household.

Based on Regina's information, Ray'Shawn had a nasty drug and drinking habit. Sometimes the drugs caused him to react violently, and Nicole found herself fleeing the house sometimes with all the children for safety until Ray'Shawn's highs came down. Carmen and Rochelle's homes had become safe havens for Nicole and her children.

One night, Ray'Shawn went too far and spanked Kent Jr. When Nicole stepped in, he ended up beating her almost as bad as he had done Layla. Carmen took her to the hospital and Rochelle kept Kent Jr. while Ray'Anna and Ray'Shawn Jr. stayed with Carmen.

Rochelle knew her cousin was becoming more dangerous, and it would only be a matter of time before Nicole would end up dead. The violence, drinking, and drugs made Nicole gravitate back to Mitchell and was now spending more time away from her children.

One day, Rochelle sat in her condo on the rug watching Kent Jr play. He had been at her house for two weeks and she felt sorry for him. Nicole was recovering from another brutal beating that resulted in the miscarriage of their second child. Ray'Shawn had made it clear that Kent Jr. was no longer welcomed into his house. Nicole asked Rochelle to keep him in hopes Ray'Shawn would come around.

Rochelle was concerned about Kent Jr.'s safety and did not want to take him back home. But in the same breath, she didn't want to be a parent yet. She continued to sit, contemplating on calling Kent.

She knew it would violate her relationship with her friend. But this point, the safety of the child she had been taking care of mattered more. She took in a deep breath and dialed Simone's phone number; they were still associating despite their sides of this scenario.

Simone answered the phone in a raspy voice, "Hello?"

"Hey, Tash, this is Rochelle. I was calling because I needed to talk to..." She paused and sat on the phone for several seconds before ending the call.

"Fuck, I don't know if I should get in this," Rochelle said to herself.

Suddenly, her phone rang. It was Simone calling back. She ignored the call and stood up from the floor and began pacing. She was thinking of another way to get Kent Jr. to his father without completely exposing everything. She knew that all Kent needed was a reason to kill her cousin and she could not carry the burden of being the cause of it. However, she had to consider being held accountable for knowing a child was in danger. If something was to happen to the infant, then she would have to live with that.

The next morning, Kent was awakened by his phone vibrating. When he answered, it was Angie.

"I have Jr. with me. Rochelle called this morning and said that Nicole wanted to do visitation. She refuses to communicate with us, so she will communicate through Rochelle and allow us to keep him," said Angie in an excited voice.

Kent sat up on the edge of his bed and looked around his bedroom to make sure he was not dreaming. After gathering himself he spoke, "I am on my way."

He stood from his bed and started scrambling around the room getting dressed. All the noise awakened Simone who sat up in bed. She began rubbing her protruding belly. She was now six months pregnant with Kent's twin son and daughter.

"Baby, is everything okay?" she questioned, witnessing Kent slip into some sweatpants and a t-shirt.

"Yes, I think so, something crazy just happened and Nicole had a change of heart. She is allowing me to see my son," said Kent, now slipping his feet into his Vapor Max tennis shoes, not caring about socks.

Simone thought about the phone call from Rochelle the day before. She wondered if that was the reason why she was calling. She would wait for Kent to leave and call Rochelle back and find out what was going on.

Simone was hearing a lot of hearsay about Nicole creeping around town with a new man. Along with witnessing Ray'Shawn at a local diner high of PCP and acting crazy, she knew things were falling apart. But she needed real confirmation. She picked up her cell and texted Rochelle asking her to meet her for lunch at the Legend of Asia in Blue Springs.

Ten minutes later, Rochelle replied, "Yes."

Simone liked the message and laid back down in bed. She would rest for another hour before getting ready to meet Rochelle.

At a local bar, Jarvis sat next to Mitchell watching the news on the big screen.

"Jarvis, I have respect for you. You're young out here but you carry yourself very well in these streets. I just want to give you your props. Despite the rivalry against my nephew and your brother, I just want to let you know there is nothing but respect. Hell, who can control our family all the time?" said Mitchell before taking his shot.

"I appreciate that coming from an OG that's been out in these streets surpassing the live expectancy of the average street nigga. Unfortunately, one of the kryptonite's of being a street nigga is pussy," responded Jarvis, taking his shot and spotting the bartender to send another round.

The two men laughed at his remark.

"Well, I'm going to head out of here. I guess I will run into you at one of these bars as we always do. But next time, rounds on me," said Mitchell, taking the last shot.

Jarvis nodded and continued watching television.

He and Mitchell could coexist in the city because they were chameleons. They came from different hoods but they only represented money and power. They knew that to be a king meant to know how to be anywhere at any time and respect everyone until disrespected.

Jarvis was born and raised right off 27th street in Kansas City, but he would not allow a neighborhood to keep him at a certain level. Whereas his brother Kent was out being loyal to the hood and gang banging. Jarvis was going to school and hustling alone in the darkness of the night.

While Kent could be found at all the best clubs and hangout spots, Jarvis was at the small places, low-key hanging with the old-heads and goats of the city. Jarvis was content with his status in life. You had to be a chess player to know that he was an important piece on the board, and he preferred for it to be that way.

At Legends of Asia, Rochelle sat patiently waiting for Simone to return from the buffet. When she entered the private eating area, Rochelle watched her as she waddled over to the table balancing two plates of food.

"Damn, you look like you are about to give birth any day now," said Rochelle.

"Girl, I feel like it, but I am only in my second trimester. I am carrying twins and the doctors say I may not make it full term," responded Simone before shoving a spoon full of rice into her mouth.

"Well, that explains everything. So, I assume you asked me to lunch because of the call you received from me last night?" questioned Rochelle.

"Yes, this morning Kent told me that Nicole had a change of heart. Not trying to be nosey, but I need to know what's going on," said Simone.

Rochelle took a deep breath; she was not sure if she should share any information with Simone. But she still held a level of trust with her. If she could help Kent Jr. out of danger, then she would take a chance and have a conversation.

Before she could open her mouth, Simone spoke again, "Look, I know this puts you in a complicated position because Ray'Shawn is your family and the fact that I am with Kent now. But please remember that I was you and Nicole's friend first and that should hold some type of weight. We both know how Nicole was and right now, I see the same manipulating person. The only difference is that she has now crossed the wrong men and children are involved."

Both women could agree that Nicole had one goal in life, to find a fine, balling ass nigga to live off his money and look good for her haters. But instead, she failed and developed a reputation of being a hoe.

"So, do you think Kent Jr. is in danger?" questioned Simone, putting another spoonful of fried rice into her mouth.

Rochelle hesitated before speaking, "That's my cousin and I don't think his intention is to harm a child. But between the drugs and his rage behind this situation, I feel he could be pushed."

"I just don't understand why Nicole won't allow Kent to take his son. He and his family, including myself, are willing to take care of Jr.," responded Simone.

Rochelle shook her head. "Girl, now you know Nicole is using that baby as a pawn to get under Kent's skin. In fact, I think the whole relationship between she and my cousin is to spite Kent."

Simone nodded in agreement; she knew that Nicole was scorn from a previous failed relationship. To see Kent happy and with someone else still bothered her and she took her frustration out on her child's father every chance she could.

The ladies finished their meals before going to the mall to do some shopping. They were happy to be able to enjoy each other's company and catch up.

TRUE LOVE

Moving forward, getting away from Ray'Shawn had become one of Nicole's daily tasks. She sat inside the dope house checking her watch every five minutes. Finally, the text she had been waiting for displayed across her screen. She smiled and hurried to the bathroom to make sure her hair was in order through the dingy mirror.

Nicole still felt battered and sore from the last fight she had with Ray'Shawn. That would not stop her from spending time with her new man. She hoped the black eye she was sporting fueled her new man to leave his wife and take her away.

Mitchell parked his van in the alley way behind one of his trap houses on the northeast side of the city. He fired up some weed and gave his horn two honks.

Moments later, Nicole came out of the back door of the spot, hurrying into the van. As soon as she closed the door, she leaned over and planted a kiss on his lips and smiled.

Mitchell removed her sunglasses, revealing her black eye and shook his head. "Man, so why didn't you call Carmen or Rochelle last night?" he questioned.

Nicole took the weed and began smoking, not offering a response.

Mitchell shook his head, started the van, and drove down the alley. They took the hour drive to Higginsville, Missouri to their secret spot at Arcadian Moon Winery. Mitchell went inside to the dining area, then ordered drinks and some samplers. Nicole was in the ladies' room freshening up. When she found the table, she took a seat. Mitchell noticed that she applied makeup to conceal the black eye.

They enjoyed the music and drinks while snacking on the appetizers. Nicole had to admit, she always felt happy and secure with Mitchell. He was always a gentleman with her. Nicole loved the power that came with Mitchell, he was one of the men in the city people referred to as the goat. He knew all the important people not just in the streets but in the community. Her only issue was that Mitchell was married. That was a constant reminder that they would never really be together.

She wondered how another woman's man could keep her cup so full. Mitchell had the ability to balance all angles of his life. He kept his wife happy, money in his pocket, and took care of his responsibilities. His wife's idea of having an open relationship gave him passes to comfortably mingle with other women. Mitchell tried not to wear the privilege out, so he was selective of the type of women he chose. His wife had one rule: play hard and don't bring anything or one to their home.

He didn't want anyone to know about the affair, so he facilitated it by taking Nicole on small weekend trips or bed and breakfast venues at least an hour away. Since he could not take her in public due to her injuries, they enjoyed the live band and drinks for a couple hours before ordering more food and heading to their hotel room to relax. They ended up making love for a couple more hours before enjoying the peace and quiet.

"I can see myself living like this forever," said Nicole, laying on the bed naked while Mitchell sat at the table rolling more weed.

Her words had taken him by surprised. He now worried if she was falling and looking forward to a future.

"Oh, is that right? Please elaborate more," he questioned.

Nicole smiled and looked over at him as if he did not know what she meant. Mitchell had been treating her perfect since they met. She was sure that meant he was planning to leave his wife for her one day because of how he handled her. She never had a man respect, wine, dine, satisfy her mentally, and physically.

"I mean spending the rest of my life with you. I am so happy and ready to leave everything behind," said Nicole, now sitting up on the bed.

Mitchell dreaded this moment. He was enjoying spending time with Nicole, but he had no plans on leaving Carmen. He knew that even if he wanted to be with her, it would not be possible because of Ray'Shawn. Despite the conversation he had with his nephew about he and Nicole, he still worried even though Ray'Shawn claimed he did not care.

His nephew ensured him that he was only messing with Nicole to get under Kent's skin. But deep-down, Ray'Shawn was falling for her. He abused her because he hated that he had falling for a hoe and knew she still loved Kent.

Mitchell could tell that his nephew had developed strong feelings. But as much as it made him feel bad, he had to admit that he was stuck on Nicole also. She was convenient, pretty, and could keep him satisfied in the bedroom. He understood how men got caught up with a girl like her. Her green eyes, milk skin, and perfect body made it easy to continue the affair. But she would never be enough to make him leave his queen Carmen because she was his true love.

They had been in love since the first day they met and conquered everything together. They got money and was always building. She was the only woman he trusted. He admired her open mind and how she always had his back.

It was Carmen's idea to make their relationship open to keep things exciting. At first, Mitchell thought it was a joke until Carmen brought home a woman one night for him.

Then a man walked in and wrapped his arms around Carmen. Mitchell had cheated on her in the past with women but was not sure if he could handle another man enjoying her. When Carmen saw his reaction, she gave the man and woman their money and instructed them to leave. They ended up making love all night. At that time, Mitchell was not open to his wife being with another man. He confirmed to Carmen that he had some insecurities. She had no intentions on sleeping with another man. She just wanted Mitchell to have freedom so that cheating would not be the downfall of their relationship.

Carmen kept the relationship open. It took Mitchell a while to step out in fear she would do the same. But when he saw Nicole at Juneteenth, he wanted her.

Everything would go smooth if he followed the rules of the open relationship. But now, things were complicated because Nicole knew Carmen and had been in their home.

"Damn, she gave a nigga a pass and I still fucked it up," mumbled Mitchell, taking a drag of the weed.

Nicole gave him a questioning look. She could tell that what she said threw off the vibe. She had a history of being rejected so she could smell it a mile away. "Look, Nicole, you know we're not moving further than the hotel rooms, movies, dinners, and just having fun. You know who my wife is, and I don't plan on ending that," said Mitchell, anticipating her reaction.

Nicole was taken aback by his words. She refused to believe that he did not want to leave his wife for her. She was determined to change his mind once she broke things off with Ray'Shawn.

She sighed, nodded her head, and appeared to be understanding in the situation. But deep down, she felt like a knife was stabbing her in the chest.

They spent the remainder of the evening making love to each other. Things were intense as they explored each other with a new lens. Mitchell ravished her body knowing that it could be the last time he would be with her. When finished, they slept for a couple hours before getting ready to go back to the city.

After the shower, they got dressed and hit the road. The ride home was quiet. Mitchell didn't want to say anything that would spark a conversation about forever. So, he turned the radio station to 103.3 and turned the volume up so that silence would not drive him crazy.

In the passenger seat, Nicole sat quietly scheming on what she was going to do to make Mitchell want to be with her. She would start with eliminating the hurdles which were Kent, Ray'Shawn, and Carmen. As she road in silence, she created a plan for Kent and Ray'Shawn. She would need her mother's help with executing it.

As for Carmen, Nicole recognized that she would be a hard obstacle to eliminate. She sat back and thought about how successful and known Carmen was. Nicole was intimidated because she carried so much substance. Carmen was like the Beyoncé of her world and Nicole had nothing to compete with other than her beauty.

Once she seen the sign, "Welcome to Kansas City", Nicole instructed Mitchell to drop her off at her apartment. Mitchell gave her a questioning look but did not object to her instruction. He just wanted to get rid of her and move on. The less confrontation, the better.

When they parked in the parking spot, Mitchell didn't bother to place the car in park.

Nicole opened the door without saying a word. She gracefully made her way up the walkway to her apartment door. When she made it to the door, she used her key to unlock it, then entered. She found her mother on the couch eating popcorn and watching television. She closed the door, kicked off her shoes, and joined her mother on the couch.

Regina stopped eating her food and gave her a look of confusion. "Umm, what's going on with you?" she asked.

"Nothing, I just decided to come home. It's time for some changes to be made. And where did you get this couch from?" responded Nicole.

"Well, does those changes include me being homeless? And a friend gave it to me. She was remodeling and was planning on taking it to the goodwill. She gave me a couple of twin beds and a king size bed," said Regina.

Nicole laughed before answering, "No, mother, I am just tired of these same rollercoasters with these men and it's time for me to make some changes that will be beneficial for my children."

Regina gave her daughter a suspicious look as she continued to eat her popcorn. Nicole stood up and headed to her bedroom, closing the door behind her. She laid down on the bed and stared at the ceiling. She thought through her plan over again to make sure it would be fool proof.

It was 3:00 am. Mitchell sat at the bar watching Carmen put the glasses away. He had arrived in time for her to close their small bar and grill called Karmin's. She had been successfully running it for over five years.

Ever since dropping off Nicole at her apartment, Mitchell could feel something in the pit of his stomach. He figured he better come clean now because Nicole probably had a plan to try and sabotage his marriage.

"Baby, we need to talk," said Mitchell.

Carmen rolled her eyes and grabbed the bottle of Jamerson before turning around. She placed the bottle on the counter and grabbed two glasses. She placed ice inside before she poured the liquor. Finally, she slid Mitchell the glass, giving him a look of conviction. She could tell by the tone of his voice that he had fucked up.

Mitchell did not waste any time trying to sugarcoat it because he knew Carmen hated that. "I've been fucking Nicole for a long time. Tonight, she gave me a couple vibes that she was trying to do more. I let her know I was not looking for that. It was something about her energy afterwards that didn't settle well with me. I feel like she probably has something up her sleeve and I just wanted to let you know so you won't be surprised."

Carmen watched him gulp his drink down. She was disappointed that he would be so messy. Of all the women he could have, he chose a hoe that was playing house with her nephew to get under another man's skin.

She shook her head at Mitchell before speaking, "This was the messiest thing you could ever do on many levels. You have that uneasy feeling because she is not finished with you like you think you are with her. Stay tuned, she most definitely has something up her sleeve and you better hope it's something that does not require me to kill her."

Carmen's words made a pit form in Mitchell's stomach. His wife was a stone-cold killer. Bringing Carmen out of retirement was not what he wanted but Nicole's next move would make that determination. Mitchell knew his wife was right, Nicole was too humble after their conversation and that meant she was plotting on how to keep him. He would keep his eye on her and hope that she did not cross the line.

RETRIBUTION PART ONE: OCTOBER 2018

It was a mild day for the month of October as Kent walked out the police station with his items in a brown paper bag. He looked around and saw Simone leaning against the car feeding one of the twins.

"Baby, I can't believe this bitch did this shit," said Kent, taking his baby girl out of Simone's arms and planting kisses on her. He checked the car for their son, but he was not inside. Kent turned to Simone with concern on his face. "Where's my little guy?"

"He had a fever, so I left him with your mother. We have to stop by the pharmacy and pick up his medicine. He has an ear infection," answered Simone, grabbing the baby.

"See, I told you to stop propping those bottles up. Just take the time to hold and feed our babies," said Kent, watching her secure his daughter in the car seat.

Simone rolled her eyes, but she knew he was right because that was exactly what the doctor told her not to do.

Once everyone was inside the car, Kent started it and exited the parking lot. He had been locked up overnight for false accusations from Nicole. She stated that he had beaten her up. Once she was able to file the report, she filed for a restraining order and was able to get Kent Jr. back. Kent had not seen Nicole in months and could not believe she would file a false report.

"I have to get my little man back. This bitch playing these games to get under my skin because I don't want her," spat Kent as he drove up 38th street heading to the pharmacy.

"Yeah, Rochelle told me that Ray'Shawn was really the one that beat her up because she would not let him see his son either," responded Simone.

"I don't know why she can't move past the anger. Shit, I let it go despite the fact she is with my rival. As long as my son is fine, I am good," responded Kent.

"So how are we going to get Kent Jr. back? I don't feel comfortable with him being with his mother," questioned Simone.

"I know I have a record and she filed that fake assault shit on me. I have to wait on the court date and plead my case. I have a meeting with the lawyer in the morning," finished Kent, parking in the pharmacy line.

Simone knew her next question would be risky. But after learning that Ray'Shawn was dealing with the same manipulating Nicole, she had to ask. "How would you feel about talking to Ray'Shawn? Maybe you two—"

Before she could finish Kent cut her off, "Baby, once you pull a gun out on a nigga, there will never be a real conversation after that." He pulled up to the pharmacy drive thru.

After picking up the prescription, they stopped by Gates Barbeque. They picked up a couple presidential platters before heading to Kent's mom's house for the evening. Kent planned to relax and wait on his meeting with his lawyer in the morning to resolve the false allegations Nicole filed. Meanwhile, Nicole was blowing his phone up. He ignored her per advice from his family and lawyer.

At home, Nicole sat looking out her window. She watched Ray'Shawn park his car in the parking spot. He got out with flowers and Chinese food, heading to the front door.

Before he could knock, Nicole opened the front door sporting the two black eyes he had given her two nights ago. When Ray'Shawn saw the damage, he shook his head remembering how he had beaten Layla.

Over the past couple days, he had been thinking about his actions. His aunt and uncle had always been looking out for him. All he had to do was stay clean and live his best life.

Despite his original motive to use Nicole to get under Kent's skin, his son, Ray'Shawn Jr., was now in the picture, and he wanted to show him something different. It was now time to make a change for the better. So, he would make things work with Nicole. He figured they both had a horrible past so the two of them could start off fresh.

"Can we talk in the bedroom?" he asked Nicole after he sat the food down on the kitchen counter.

Nicole led the way to her bedroom. When they entered, he closed the door and handed her the roses.

"Look, I know this won't take the pain away, but for what it's worth, I am sorry. I want to move forward and make things better for us," said Ray'Shawn.

Nicole did not respond. Ray'Shawn was now old news because she wanted Mitchell. She sniffed the roses and smiled. "Well, let's just chill here and take it one day at a time." She placed the roses on the window seal and exited the bedroom.

Ray'Shawn smiled and took off his jacket. He went to the second bedroom to see his son.

Nicole made her way to the kitchen where her mother was already eating the Chinese food. "Momma, remember the plan? It's time for you to do your part in a couple hours," whispered Nicole, making sure Ray'Shawn was not around.

Regina dropped her fork on the plate and rolled her eyes before answering, "Ray'Shawn seems like he is trying to make it work. Why not just give it a chance? Try to be happy with him and let Kent father his son. This just might work better than this plan you conjured up."

"Well, if you want a place to live, you better agree," said Nicole, giving her mother a serious look.

That evening, everyone watched movies. Instead of smoking PCP, Ray'Shawn rolled up a couple of blunts for them to smoke. They ordered more food, this time pizza. They fed the children before laying them down for

173

bed. A couple hours later, Ray'Shawn was asleep in bed and Nicole laid next to him trying to fall asleep.

As planned, Regina went outside and dialed Kent's phone number and waited for an answer. It was midnight and the phone rung several times before he answered in a raspy voice.

"Kent, I need you to come quick! Ray'Shawn on bullshit again and this time he hit Kent Jr.," whispered Regina, smoking a cigarette.

Kent didn't say anything. He just hung up the phone and got out of bed. He dressed without saying anything to Simone who woke up and sat on the edge of the bed confused. He grabbed his car keys and drove over to Nicole's apartment. Nicole and Regina acted as if they were asleep as Kent beat on the door, waking Ray'Shawn out of his sleep.

"Who the fuck beating on the door like that," said Ray'Shawn, grabbing his gun and heading downstairs to the front door.

Before he could reach the door, Kent kicked it in causing Ray'Shawn to point his weapon. Both men aimed and fired several shots at each other, not missing their target. When Regina and Nicole made it downstairs, they found both Kent and Ray'Shawn laid out dead.

"Oh, my lord! Nicole, was this your plan?" shouted Regina, smacking her daughter.

Nicole smirked and grabbed her jaw before speaking in a monotone voice, "What's wrong, mom? Isn't this what you and my aunt wanted? For me to be ruthless."

Nicole could hear the police sirens. She began to cry before turning and running outside, appearing to look frantic for her neighbors.

At that moment, Regina realized that she and her sister had ruined her baby girl. She sat at the foot of the stairs and looked at both Kent's and Ray'Shawn's bodies lying bloody on the living room floor. Both of their eyes were still open staring into nothing. Their lifeless bodies reminded Regina of the night she had killed Nicole's father.

She told her daughter that she did not know who her father was. But the truth was she had set him up to die the night she conceived Nicole. Regina began to cry, and her sobriety went out the window. She was going to get a hit after this was over.

At home, Simone screamed when she heard Rochelle on the other end of the phone telling her that Kent was dead. She hurried to the hospital. She met up with Angie, Jarvis, and Kent's mother who were in the waiting area crying.

"I told this nigga to leave her alone," said Jarvis unable to contain himself. He began beating the wall, causing security to come into the waiting area.

"Don't worry we have him under control," said Angie's husband to the security guards. The guards nodded and exited the area.

When the Chaplin arrived, they all followed her to the room where Kent's lifeless body laid covered from the neck down.

After saying a prayer with the Chaplin, Jarvis stood over his brother's body and grabbed the sheet. When he pulled it off his brother, the bullet wounds were on display. Angie screamed and ran out the room while their mother stood over her son, her eyes wide and mouth covered.

"I'm sorry, mom, but I never want to forget what happened to my brother," said Jarvis. He turned and exited the room.

At another hospital, Carmen, Mitchell, and Rochelle stood, looking down and Ray'Shawn's lifeless body. Nicole laid on the floor crying in the hallway.

"I can't believe this shit happened. He was just talking about getting things right," said Carmen.

"Something is not right. I can feel it. The story does not make sense," said Mitchell.

"That's what I say, pops," responded Rochelle.

They all stood around Ray'Shawn's body for several minutes. The silence in the room was so loud that Rochelle could no longer take it, so she left the room.

Carmen looked at her husband and spoke, "You see how dangerous these bitches are. This shit has set up all over it."

Mitchell looked down at his nephew. He began to think of memories of Ray'Shawn as a child. He remembered when Carmen brought him home and said they were going to take care of him. Mitchell was young but that did not stop him from learning to be a father. He treated Ray'Shawn like a son, teaching him everything he knew about the game. Ray'Shawn was destined to fall in Mitchell's footsteps until he developed a drug habit, snorting cocaine and smoking PCP. Things began to turn for the worse.

Mitchell and Carmen tried to gain a grip on Ray'Shawn. They supported him and hoped that showing him the finer things in life would make him fall back in line. But it did not work, and Ray'Shawn was more drawn to living reckless. He met Layla and within months, she was pregnant with his daughter, Ray'Anna. Despite the age of the young couple, Mitchell and Carmen felt it would settle Ray'Shawn down.

But the beautiful baby girl only helped make things better for a little while. By the time Ray'Anna was six months, Ray'Shawn was back on drugs. He began to spend more time having fun with the homies and spending his money irresponsibly. When the money began to run low, and Carmen stopped catering to him, Ray'Shawn began hustling on the streets to support his habit and lifestyle.

He moved in with Layla and things were going well until she started sleeping around with Kent and stripping. The day that Kent came to Layla's apartment was Ray'Shawn's breaking point.

Mitchell sobbed as he stood over Ray'Shawn. "You were the only son I ever had. Don't worry, I got you and your seeds, I promise," he whispered before leaving the room.

A Week Later

The deaths of both Kent and Ray'Shawn was the talk of the town. On social media, everyone had their opinions and theories about what happened. Nicole played the victim posting on social media saying how she missed her fiancé Ray'Shawn and that they were planning on moving out of Kansas City. She earned the sympathy of her audience.

The death investigation concluded that Kent was the aggressor for kicking in the front door forcing Ray'Shawn to defend himself. The media described it as a standoff between two men fighting for Nicole's heart.

As time passed, the streets began to put things together and Nicole was no longer considered a victim. She had to go into hiding and deactivate her social media pages because she was being harassed and receiving death threats. She was being accused of setting Kent and

Ray'Shawn up. Things got so bad that Tanisha's house was broken into and ransacked, causing her to live out of a hotel room.

After making several attempts to contact Mitchell, he finally surfaced. Nicole convinced him to take her to a safe place. He picked her and the children up in the middle of the night and drove to Maryville, Missouri. He set them up in one of his properties he had just remodeled to flip.

When Nicole entered the home and turned on the lights, she was convinced that Mitchell had this house waiting for her. It had everything she wanted and needed, and the décor was identical to her taste. As she walked through the house, she could tell that Mitchell had been listening to her during pillow talk and that meant a lot to her.

Mitchell took a seat on the brand-new couch and observed Nicole checking out the house. It pissed him off that she had completely forgotten about how distraught she was about Ray'Shawn's death, and he wasn't in the ground yet.

"Hey, I am going to order out for the kids. There are not many places in this small town unless you want to go to Applebee's. It's not far away," said Mitchell, sitting at the edge of the couch.

Nicole turned to him and nodded. She noticed the sadness in his eyes. Seeing him hurting made her feel a little guilt, but her plan was working and that's all that mattered.

"Let's go to Applebee's," she answered before rounding the kids up and heading out the door to the van.

Mitchell took a moment and sat on the couch while Nicole loaded Kent and Ray'Shawn inside the car. He did not want to be here because his family was at home mourning. His wife was not doing well and Ray'Anna had not been sleeping at night. He found himself wishing that Nicole was the one dead instead. All he could play in his head was Ray'Shawn's bullet riddled body and Carmen blaming him. Some days,

Carmen was not able to get out of bed nor leave the house. So, Rochelle was running the bar and grill per Mitchell's request.

Mitchell got wrapped in his thoughts. He could not believe he was helping the woman that was responsible for it all. If it wasn't for his wife's request to stay close to Ray'Shawn Jr., he would have been done with Nicole. He knew it was also a punishment for getting the family in a messy situation.

Mitchell's thoughts were disturbed by Nicole tapping him on the shoulder. "Hey, I have the kids in the car. Are you okay? We can order out or something if you're not feeling it," she spoke in a low soft voice.

"No, its fine, let's get out and feed these kids," said Mitchell, standing up.

He forced himself to plant a kiss on Nicole's forehead before making his way out of the front door. Nicole hurried behind him, closing and locking the front door first. She knew it would be rough for a while because Mitchell was grieving. But once everyone moved on with their lives, then she would have him and the family she deserved.

Later that night in Kansas City, Rochelle and Carmen knocked on the door of the trap house that appeared to be vacant. Regina opened the door and almost pissed herself to see Carmen standing before her. She remembered when Carmen used to hustle on the corner because she was her number one customer. When she was pimping, Regina was one of her best bottom bitches.

Carmen walked past Regina without saying a word and Rochelle followed, only offering a quick nod.

"Damn, I haven't seen the inside of this house in years," said Carmen, frowning at the dingy walls.

"I think you and pops can rehab this place and bring it back," joked Rochelle.

They both shared a laugh while Regina leaned against the wall smoking a cigarette. She was nervous because she knew that Carmen was the real definition of a gangster, and she never wanted to be on the opposite side of her fist or gun.

She remembered Carmen settling down when her older sister, who was Ray'Shawn's mother, died of breast cancer. She took her nephew in. He was a son to her, and she wanted to know the truth behind his tragic death.

After receiving a call from Simone informing her that Regina was the one that called Kent to the apartment that night, she knew it would be easy to get the truth.

"Look, Regina, you know why I am here. You were in the apartment the night my family died, and I want to know what really happened," said Carmen, lighting up her weed.

Regina felt her stomach knot up as both Carmen and Rochelle stared into her. Afraid, she decided to come clean. She hoped that Carmen would understand that she was just doing what her daughter asked with no idea it would get fatal.

"My daughter had me call Kent and tell him it was an emergency. I had no idea it was going to end up like this," Regina pleaded. "Look, you two have to believe me. Come on, Rochelle, I know that Mitchell is your father and I never told Nicole that. You two have to believe me when I say that I had nothing to do with what happened." Tears poured out of her eyes.

"What the fuck does Mitchell being Rochelle's father have to do with anything? And if you would have told her that, it still would not have stopped her from hoeing around with him anyway," spat Carmen.

"Why did your daughter feel the need to relocate? Leaving you and your sister here to watch each other's back. Come on, this is your chance, Regina, to come clean. We already know some set up shit went down, so confirm it," said Rochelle.

Regina wiped the tears from her eyes and lit another cigarette before speaking, "Okay, Nicole wanted to get Ray'Shawn and Kent back for treating her fucked up, so she planned to have them eliminate each other. Then she would move on and—"

Before Regina could finish her words, Carmen interrupted, "Be a family with Mitchell? You mean to tell me that you didn't put your daughter up on game? Mitchell is going nowhere, that bag is secure, believe that." She took her forty-five out and shot Regina in the chest twice.

They stood and watched her slide down the wall to the floor and die. When she took her last breath, Rochelle and Carmen exited the house as if nothing happened. They then doused the house with gasoline and set it afire. They parked at the end of the block and watched it burn until the fire department showed up. With the truth out, Carmen could now formulate a plan on what to do to Nicole.

RETRIBUTION PART TWO: TWO WEEKS LATER

Kent's funeral was held in an undisclosed location. Only family and close friends were allowed with an invite. Simone stood over the black casket staring down at the man she thought she would spend her life with. Kent was dressed traditional per his mother's request. He wore a black suit and blue tie with a matching flower in the pocket. His hair was freshly cut, and his face was shaved. Simone admired his dark complexion. Her aunt had done so well on the makeup that he looked like he was peacefully asleep.

"Don't worry, baby, I will never forget us, and I will raise our babies to be the best. We will get Kent Jr. soon, so don't worry," she whispered before planting a kiss on his lips.

Kent's cold lips made Simone break down, confirming there was no life in his body. She suddenly could feel herself becoming dizzy. She stumbled back a couple steps. Jarvis caught her and helped her to one of the seats before returning to the casket.

He looked down at his older brother and tried to fight back the tears. "Don't worry, big bro, I am going to find that bitch and kill her with my bare hands," he whispered before placing the gold cross in his brother's hand and walking away.

After the services, family and friends met up at the Ameristar hotel where Jarvis reserved two suites. He, his mother, Angie, her husband and children, Simone and the twins, and her Aunt Martha would spend the next couple days there before taking a trip to San Diego, California. They would spend a week in Jarvis's friend Alan's family beach home. Once everyone settled in the suite, Mitchell arrived.

He made a trip into town to pay his respects to Kent's family. "How are you holding up?" asked

Mitchell, sitting at the mini bar drinking Hennessey out of the bottle.

Jarvis didn't respond for several seconds. Now that the services were over and things started to wind down, it was more painful to accept his brother was gone.

"Shit feels horrible now. My brother is really gone. I have to learn to live with this shit," he responded before taking another drink.

"I know this is not much help to your situation, but I have to keep it real with you, young blood. You're still young and this is only going to be one of the worst things you will have to ever get through. Just keep your head up. That pain in your chest will fade away as time goes by," spoke Mitchell.

Jarvis nodded in agreement. "So, what's up with that bitch Nicole. She wouldn't even let us get my nephew so he could see his father one last time. I swear, when I get the chance…" Jarvis paused and took another drink from his bottle before shaking his head and allowing the tears to flow down his face. He was all over the place and had murder on his mind.

"I wouldn't worry. She is going to get her karma one way or another. I heard her mother was murdered and burned in an abandoned house a few days ago," said Mitchell, taking a drink.

"Shit, that's not enough but it's a good start. Shit, killing her quick is not enough either. I need her to be in a high place before she dies. My brother was in a high place when she snatched the rug from under him. So, I need her to feel all that shit," said Jarvis, now displaying a mincing look on his face.

"Look, remember not to act on impulse and just be patient with the process. Things will go in everyone's favor at the end. Take the family to Cali and relax and grieve. You need that for your sanity," said Mitchell.

Jarvis took another drink before responding, "Damn, you have to bury your nephew tomorrow. If I haven't said it, my condolences," said Jarvis.

Suddenly, Adam and Jarvis's homies Mike and Erin came into the room with more bottles of liquor. They spent the evening drinking, playing cards, and reminiscing about Kent. The suites were shared by a door, so Jarvis's mother opened the doors, allowing the children to roam freely.

Mitchell hung around and watched everyone enjoy each other. He tried to hold on, but the tragic situation was taking a toll on him. Kent's twins were crawling all over the place and it was sad they had no idea that they would be spending their lives without a father. Simone looked like she had a hard couple of weeks. Her brick house body seemed to have shed. She looked fragile, but she tried to hold it together by keeping busy.

Kent's mom was quiet as she sat on one of the couches and watched everyone while drinking her wine. Mitchell could tell she was still trying to accept what happened to her son. He felt compassion for the mother who had raised her children with all she had. He knew it was a devastating blow and that she felt she had failed.

He knew that a single mother's biggest accomplishment is to raise successful children and beating all odds. The odds become greater once the father walks away. Mitchell remembered his mother raising him all by herself. It took strength and sacrifice to make things happen. He respected a woman that had perseverance.

The next day, Nicole rented a car and drove back to Kansas City after receiving a call from her aunt about her mother. When she arrived, she picked up her aunt, and they drove to the funeral home to arrange services. When they arrived, they both entered and was greeted by the secretary. When Nicole gave the woman her mother's name, she went to the back to get the owner, Mr. Jacobs, to help them. Once Mr. Jacobs was available, he escorted the women to his office.

"My condolences to you ladies and your family. My secretary stated that you wanted to view your mother's body before planning services. I want to let you know that your mother was in a fire. I must warn you that if you want to see her, it will not be a pleasant sight.

She has 3rd degree burns all over her," said Mr. Jacobs, showing a picture of her mother's arm.

Nicole's aunt snatched the picture from Mr. Jacobs and looked at it before speaking, "So, you are saying that my sister's face looks like this also?" When Mr. Jacobs nodded, Tanisha burst into tears and dropped the picture on the floor.

Nicole sat one thousand dollars on the desk and spoke, "There will be no services. I just want to see my mother before she is cremated, please."

Mr. Jacobs nodded, stood from his desk, and exited the office. He instructed his staff to prepare Regina to the best to their ability. The stylist covered her body from the neck down. Then wrapped her head because her hair had burned away. Fifteen minutes later, Mr. Jacobs returned and escorted Nicole to one of the viewing areas to see her mother.

"Take as much time as you need. I will gather the paperwork and get your receipt," spoke Mr. Jacobs before leaving Nicole in the room with one of his staff members.

Nicole stood over the loaner coffin and looked at her mother's burned face. Her eye lids were gone, and one of her eyes, so it was covered by a patch. The smell of burnt flesh invaded her nostrils but she endured the odor. Despite the strained relationship with her mother, Nicole felt sadness and guilt. She knew that she was the cause of her mother's death and regretted involving her. She knew that Jarvis was behind all of this, as revenge for his brother's death.

"Goodbye, mother," said Nicole before walking out the sanctuary. She headed back to Mr. Jacobs's office to sign the paperwork.

"The cremains will be ready in two weeks for pick up. Here are your two copies of the death certificates. I am always happy to be able to find the family in this type of situation. We work with the county morgue to resolve bodies that are not claimed," finished Mr. Jacobs.

Nicole took the certificates and helped Tanisha out of her seat. They hurried out of the funeral home. The children waited in the van still asleep. Once inside, Nicole looked at the death certificate. She read that the cause of death was gunshots to the chest. She returned the certificate to the envelope and started the car before driving out of the parking lot.

As she drove, she tried to drown out Tanisha's sobbing. She thought about Ray'Shawn's funeral services that would start in one hour. She wanted to show her face, but she knew that she would not be welcomed. She found it strange that Ray'Shawn's family did not request for his son to attend like Kent's family had done. In her eyes, that was a sign that she was in danger along with her aunt.

"Auntie, I am going to take you back to my new place. I don't think it is safe here," said Nicole.

Tanisha looked up before speaking, "No, thank you, I know you set those nigga's up to die because Regina told me. Now look, she is dead, and you think you are safe? Shit, at this point, I don't want to be anywhere near you. Now that she is dead, I don't want to be nowhere near you. Just drop me off at the bus station. I am going down south like I should have done years ago."

Tanisha's words hurt but Nicole did not object to the request. Once her aunt was gone, she could go back to Maryville and continue her life with Mitchell and the boys. She would never look back at Kansas City.

When Nicole parked in front of the bus station, Tanisha exited the car without saying goodbye. Nicole sat for a moment crying, hoping her aunt would come back and at least say goodbye and that she loved her. But after fifteen minutes passed, she drove away. She headed to the church where Ray'Shawn's services were being held. She sat outside watching everyone going in and out. She cried when she saw the blood red coffin being carried by Mitchell and five other men exit the church. After everyone drove away in the procession, she took note of the funeral home before driving away. She would head home and review his program online.

Once at the cemetery, everyone huddled around Ray'Shawn's coffin while the funeral director spoke.

"Ashes to ashes, dust to dust. The family of Ray'Shawn Cummings would like to thank everyone for their condolences and kind gestures in their time of grief. The repast will be held at Karmin's," said the funeral director.

Everyone grabbed one of the roses from Ray'Shawn's coffin and headed to their cars except for Carmen, Rochelle, and Mitchell.

"Rochelle, head over to Karmin's. Mitchell and I will be right behind you," said Carmen.

Rochelle nodded and went to Carmen's red Camaro. She got inside and drove away. Mitchell stood watching Carmen staring at the coffin for several minutes before he intervened.

"Baby, we should head over to the repast," said Mitchell in a low voice.

"I want you to stay in Maryville until I figure out what I am going to do," said Carmen, never taking her eyes away from the coffin.

The words of staying in Maryville with Nicole made Mitchell's heart drop. "Baby, no, I am staying here with my family. We all need to be together. Don't worry, I have that bitch wrapped around my finger. I don't need to be there with her every day!" yelled Mitchell.

Carmen turned around with tears in her eye. "Yes, you will go there and be with my fucking nephew until I figure things out. Come on now, it was not hard when you were laying up with her. Do you realize she probably would not have set my nephew up if she were not stuck on you? I spoke to her mother, and she told me that Nicole wanted to be a family with you and you two discussed plans to move away!" shouted Carmen.

"That pillow talk shit doesn't mean anything. We were just kicking it. I just want to keep her close until we can get Ray'Shawn Jr., that's it," countered Mitchell.

"You go stay with that bitch until I say stop and that's it. I don't need you here to console me, I need revenge on the bitch that caused the death of my nephew."

"Well, just let me put a bullet in her head and be done with the shit," said Mitchell, now following Carmen to his truck.

Carmen waited for him to open the passenger door and she got inside the truck. Before Mitchell closed the door, she spoke, "Placing a bullet in her head is too easy, I could have done that. The police are all over this shit. It would bring too much heat on both Kent family and ours if Nicole came up dead."

Mitchell didn't object, he just wanted it all to be over so he could be with his family. When they made it to Karmin's, it was packed. They went inside and Rochelle was behind the bar pouring her father a drink.

"Pops, is everything okay?" questioned Rochelle.

Mitchell spoke, never taking his eyes off his wife. She was sitting at one of the tables talking with some family members. "No, baby, it's not okay and I don't know when it will be."

For the remainder of the day, Rochelle continued to watch her father and stepmother. It hurt her to see the only mother she had ever known hurting. Her father being in a bad situation having to deal with Nicole angered her. She grabbed her phone and texted Jarvis, telling him to meet with her when he returned from California.

LIFE GOES ON: JANUARY 2020

Mitchell sat on the back patio drinking a glass of Hennessy White, admiring the white snow that covered everything. It was twenty degrees outside, but the liquor, North Face coat, and heating lamp made it easy to stand. It had been over a year since he had buried Ray'Shawn.

Carmen would not let him come back home and kept the conversations short and simple. Mitchell was convinced his wife did not want him anymore. It hurt at the thought of living without her. He maintained small hope that it was all a part of the plan.

The only joy he had was watching both boys growing up and enjoying life without a care in the world. He often wished that he could have had children with his wife. Carmen was so invested in Ray'Shawn, that she did not want any children. Mitchell resented his wife for only considering her wants and that's why he started cheating in the past. Then when she found out that he was, she took control of the situation by opening the relationship instead of listening to his cry for help.

His thoughts were disturbed by Nicole coming out on the patio to check on him. Mitchell had to admit, Nicole would have made an exceptionally good housewife. She was clean, cooked, was not a pest, kept herself up, took care of the children, and kept him sexually satisfied. But he was ready for his wife to call him back home.

"Hey, I am going to head to bed, did you need anything?" Nicole waited for his response.

"No, I will be in shortly. Are the boys asleep already?" asked Mitchell.

"Yep, that trip to the park to sled wore them out," responded Nicole before going back inside.

As soon as the coast was clear, Jarvis stepped onto the patio and took a seat in one of the empty chairs. He wore all black and had his hood over his head, concealing his face just in case Nicole came back outside.

"Damn, nigga, where the hell you come from?" questioned Mitchell, looking around.

Jarvis looked at the door before speaking, "Shit, I live right across the street. I been up here since you moved her up here, just chilling waiting on that moment to strike."

"Shit, I am starting to think it's no longer a plan," said Mitchell.

"Come on, OG, you have moved up here and started playing family man. The plan is still on, we just needed time to pass," answered Jarvis, standing up from the chair. He gestured for Mitchell to follow.

Jarvis led him to the house next door. He tapped on the door three times. When the door opened, there stood Carmen. Mitchell looked at his wife from head to toe, she had slimmed.

"Baby," said Mitchell, embracing his wife.

Jarvis stood and watched them hold each other for several minutes before taking a seat on the couch.

"Baby, what the fuck? I didn't know what was happening to us. You had not called me or accepted any calls," said Mitchell, holding her hand.

"I won't lie, I was in my feeling about everything. I needed distance from you to clear my mind. I also needed to think about how I was going to deal with this situation. I won't lie, I missed you many days, but I had to be strong so that we could finish this shit," said Carmen.

Mitchell kissed his wife; her lips was just as soft as he remembered. She smiled and a tear ran down her eye. "Shit, I thought Nicole was going to snatch your heart from me. But I had to risk it to get the job done," said Carmen.

Suddenly, they were disturbed by the sound of the garage door opening. It was Rochelle parking the van inside. Jarvis opened the door leading to the garage, letting Rochelle inside. When Mitchell saw her large belly, he smiled and went over to her. He hugged her and planted kisses on her face.

"Oh, this is a wonderful surprise. This must be the grandson I have been waiting for," said Mitchell, placing his hand on her belly.

Rochelle smiled and nodded. Mitchell turned around to Jarvis and Carmen.

"Okay, so what's the mutha-fuckin plan? I am ready to get back to my family."

For the next two hours, Carmen ran the plan down to Mitchell while Jarvis smoked, and Rochelle snacked while watching television. When everything was explained, Mitchell returned to the home he shared with Nicole and laid on the couch in the dark. He did not want to go sleep with Nicole because Carmen being next door was on his mind. He wanted to make love to her.

The next morning, Nicole awakened to find Mitchell had not been in bed at all. The smell of bacon invaded her nostrils as she headed down the hall into the living room and to the kitchen where she found him.

Nicole took a seat and looked around. She had not seen Mitchell cook breakfast since she had known him. It made her think to herself, *maybe he's coming around.* She had been working hard to keep him satisfied the last few months, trying to prove to him that he made the right decision by staying with her.

Mitchell served Nicole a plate of bacon, scrambled eggs with cheese, French toast, and cranberry juice. He then took a seat across the table with his plate and began eating.

Nicole enjoyed her breakfast but realized the children had not come out yet. "I wonder why the boys are not up yet," she stated.

Mitchell looked up. "Remember that daycare center we were talking about? I took them there earlier. It's time to start socializing them so they can be ready for school. Plus, you need a break so enjoy it," he said, putting his fork down.

He watched Nicole finish her breakfast. After taking her last bite, he spoke again, "You know, you definitely stood by your word and proved to me that you were wifey material."

Nicole's face lit up; she knew what this moment meant. Her fair skin blushed as he continued to speak, "I know what you are thinking. I can tell by the way your face is lighting up." Mitchell teased, taking a drink of his Hennessy and orange juice.

"I don't want to say it, I want to hear you say it," said Nicole, standing from the table and walking over to him.

Mitchell watched her saunter over to him wearing one of his favorite Victoria Secret gowns. She sat on his lap and began sucking on his bottom lip. Mitchell could feel his man hood rising but had to continue the plan.

"You know, it sounds crazy, but you know I am from down south. And one of the things I always wanted to do was get married in a barn. I have the location in Louisiana. Do you think you can plan something in two weeks?" questioned Mitchell, sliding his hands between her legs.

"Yes, two weeks. I can do it," moaned Nicole, enjoying Mitchell pleasing her with his finger. He smacked her thigh and pointed to the bedroom and Nicole led the way.

For the next week, Nicole spent time planning her wedding. She did not care that she had no family to invite. She reached out to her friend Rochelle; they had been distant since Ray'Shawn's death.

Rochelle agreed to assist with traveling down to the venue to make sure everything was going as planned. "Girl, I will be back up in a couple days. I will transport the kids down so you and your future husband can have a wonderful road trip," said Rochelle as she laid in her living room flicking the television remote.

"Rochelle, I am so excited, and I can't believe you are pregnant! So, this means I am going to be a god mother," said Nicole, giving the boys a bath.

"Oh, yeah, I never got to formally ask you that. But, girl, you know you are the one. I need a baby shower. But look, I must answer this call. This is the photographer I found, the best one in Louisiana," she spoke into the phone. "Great, I will see you in a couple of days." Rochelle ended the call and tossed the phone on the couch.

Nicole finished giving the boys a bath and put them down to bed. She walked in the guest bedroom and checked to make sure the suitcases were packed and ready to go. On the bed inside a bag was the wedding dress she had Sheraz Pompey custom make. She unzipped the bag and admired the dress she would be wearing in the next four days.

"Can I see the dress?" said Mitchell, standing in the doorway.

Nicole hurried and turned around, blocking the dress. "No, it's bad luck to see the bride's dress before the wedding! Trust me, you will be satisfied," responded Nicole, turning around, and zipping the dress back up.

For the next couple of days, Nicole floated on air dreaming of her wedding. She had finally made it and all the men that had left her hanging would miss out because she would be a great wife. After the wedding, she and Mitchell were moving to Las Vegas to raise the boys. She stopped taking her birth control a month ago and had planned on getting pregnant. She hoped for a girl but knew that Mitchell wanted a boy of his own flesh and blood.

Two days later, Rochelle arrived and picked up Kent Jr. and Ray'Shawn Jr., while Mitchell loaded the bags in the trunk. He and Nicole watched Rochelle drive away before they finished loading the rest of their stuff for their trip to Lafayette, Louisiana.

During the ride, Nicole reviewed the pictures that Rochelle sent her of the décor as Mitchell drove quietly. They had fifteen hours to drive and would take turns until they arrived.

"Baby, I have a surprise for you," said Mitchell, pointing to the glove compartment.

Nicole opened the compartment. There was an envelope with her name written on it. When she opened it, there were divorce papers.

"You have been so high on planning the wedding, you never asked if I divorced Carmen," joked Mitchell as he continued down the road.

Nicole smiled as she reviewed the documents. The sight of Carmen's signature on the paperwork had her high on happiness. She returned the documents to the envelope and unbuckled her seatbelt.

"I know we didn't travel without the kids for nothing," flirted Nicole in a seductive voice.

Before Mitchell could respond, Nicole was unzipping his pants. She took out his manhood and began sucking. No longer able to concentrate, Mitchell pulled over alongside of the road to get one last shot of Nicole before making it to Louisiana.

Hours later, Nicole walked inside the barn. Her face lit up at the sight of the beautiful red, gold, and black décor. The alter was surrounded by red roses just as she envisioned.

Satisfied, she found her quarters and took her dress inside. She called Rochelle to make sure she was on the way with the boys. After confirming, she began to prepare. Despite the fact she had no bridesmaids and no idea who was attending her wedding, she was still happy.

Moments later, she was surprised to see her Aunt Tanisha standing in the doorway. "Auntie, how did you find out? I didn't know where to find you," said Nicole, hugging Tanisha.

Tanisha offered a smile and spoke, "Mitchell told me about it. I could not miss it for the world. I guess you were right, you were determined to become a wifey and you succeeded."

Tanisha helped her niece get dressed for her big day. When ready, they exited the dressing room. When the doors opened, it was dark. Then a spotlight shined on Nicole. She could not see anything but Mitchell and a man standing that appeared to be the preacher as she walked down the aisle.

Her favorite Mary J. Blige song, "*You Gotta Believe*", played and she wondered how many people were in the room watching her, admiring her custom-made red dress that hugged her body with the long train. She held a bouquet of white roses and wore diamonds that complemented the sparkles on the dress.

When Nicole made it to the alter, the music stopped, and Mitchell took her hand. He looked into her eyes and said to her, "You are a beautiful bride. I will never forget this vision nor this day. You have proven to me that you are the one," Mitchell paused before continuing, "but you would never amount to the woman that I am married to, you scandalous bitch." He let go of her hand and smacked her. All the blood seemed to drain from Nicole's face. She could not believe what just happened.

Suddenly, the lights came on and there stood Carmen with a gun pointed to Tanisha's head. The preacher removed his hood, revealing himself. It was Jarvis. He gave Nicole a smirk and tossed the bible at her feet. When Nicole looked back at Mitchell, his loving eyes was now dark and menacing. She began to feel dizzy and stumbled back a couple steps.

"Oh, don't get weak in the knees now, we're just beginning," said Carmen before delivering a bullet in Tanisha's head.

Nicole watched her aunt fall to the wood floor. Carmen stepped over Tanisha's body like she was trash and stepped onto the alter.

She smacked Nicole before speaking, "Bitch, did you think I was going to let you slide with killing my nephew?"

She punched her in the mouth causing Nicole to fall. Carmen did not waste any time sitting on top of her delivering punch after punch. The images of Ray'Shawn's lifeless body and Nicole sleeping with Mitchell fueled every punch. Jarvis and Mitchell stood and watched Carmen beat Nicole for several minutes until she was out of breath.

Once Carmen stood to her feet, she gestured for Jarvis to come over. He stood over Nicole and smiled before speaking, "You thought I wasn't going to come back about my brother?" He delivered a shot in both of her knees.

Nicole yelled in pain while rolling around. Suddenly, Simone appeared in the barn door. She walked down slowly with a knife in her hand. Simone had a dual revenge to handle because Nicole was the one that set her brother up. Simone stood over Nicole as she winced in pain and held out a photo of her brother Fabian.

"Remember this man? You met with him at a motel in the bottoms and sucked his dick before his rivals came inside and murdered him. That was my older brother. I have been waiting on an opportunity to get you ever since," spoke Simone.

She dropped to her knees, held the knife over her head, and came down, stabbing Nicole multiple times. When she stopped, Nicole was still alive.

"Damn, she's like a fuckin zombie or some shit," said Jarvis, standing over her aiming the gun to shoot her again.

But Mitchell stopped him, "Nah, let's take her to the swamp, the crocs like their food living."

Jarvis and Mitchell dragged Nicole's body and tossed her on the backseat of the car. Carmen got in the driver seat and Mitchell in the passenger seat.

Simone and Jarvis stayed behind while Carmen and Mitchell drove Nicole to a swamp not far from the farmhouse.

When they arrived, Carmen and Mitchell dragged Nicole to the edge of the swamp and left her for dead. They got back into the car and began driving but Carmen stopped.

She looked at her husband. "Can you believe this bitch is still alive after being beat and stabbed? Shit, I want her to die slow and suffer, but I don't want to leave her alive. What if she makes it out?"

"You're right like always, baby, let's end this. I am ready to come home," spoke Mitchell.

He exited the car and walked back down to Nicole. She was laying still, looking up to the sky smiling.

"I am glad to see you smile one more time before you die," he spoke before pulling the trigger. He pumped two bullets, one in her eye and the other in her heart.

"There is no turning back from the chest shot," Mitchell mumbled while turning away and casually walking back to the car.

He hopped inside and Carmen drove away leaving Nicole to die. When they returned to the barn, Mitchell's grandfather had some men cleaning up the mock wedding. Simone showered and Jarvis was sitting under one of the lemon trees smoking his weed.

"Don't worry about the body, those crocs will handle that before the night is over. Don't forget to torch that car, the clothing, and all items that were involved today," spoke Mitchell's grandfather before heading back into his house.

After loading Nicole's belongings, Tanisha's body, along with everyone's clothing in the car, Jarvis set it on fire. They stood under the lemon tree and watched it burn.

"I am glad this bitch is gone. It can't bring back my brother, but at least I have his seed and don't have to worry about that bitch raising him," said Jarvis, passing the weed to Mitchell.

"I agree young blood, and I am glad that I don't have to lay up with that hoe and fake anymore. I can get back to my real family," responded Mitchell before taking two puffs of the weed and passing it to Simone.

"I have been trying to figure out a strategy to get that Nicole since I found out she was the one that set my big brother up. She was always doing scandalous shit. I hate that Kent and Ray'Shawn became casualties," said Simone after hitting the weed and passing it to Carmen.

"She was no different than her mother and aunt. They have been in the setting up niggas field for years, just passing it down from generation to generation. The only thing is that Tanisha stopped after almost losing her life and Regina became a crack head," said Carmen before hitting the weed.

After the car burned out, Mitchell's father had it taken to a salvage yard, and it was destroyed. After getting a few hours of sleep Mitchell, Carmen, Jarvis, and Simone drove back to Kansas City. They stopped by Rochelle's; she was now living in Ray'Shawn's house. Jarvis and Simone took Kent Jr. home to live with their family and Ray'Shawn Jr. lived with Mitchell, Carmen, and Ray'Anna.

Mitchell was happy to be back home, but every time he looked at Ray'Shawn Jr.'s green eyes, it reminded him of Nicole. He wondered where they would be if she would have hooked up with him the night of

Juneteenth instead of getting with Kent. He found himself drifting away from time to time thinking about how she looked in the wedding dress walking down the aisle. He felt a little guilt as he imagined that Nicole lived a lonely life.

This situation taught him a valuable lesson. He did not need multiple women. The value was in family, and it was important to support each other. He hated it took a tragedy to learn this lesson. However, he gained an extended family with Kent's family. He committed to make changes for the better and knew he would have to answer to God about the role he played in Nicole's murder. He would deal with that when it came, now was the time to enjoy his life.

THE END

www.ingramcontent.com/pod-product-compliance
Lightning Source LLC
Chambersburg PA
CBHW050353030726
47503CB00006B/1840